PRAISE FOR JOSH LIEB'S *NEW YORK TIMES* BESTSELLING

★★★

I am a genius of unspeakable evil and I want to be your class president

★★★

"If *War and Peace* had a baby with *The Breakfast Club* and then left that baby to be raised by wolves, this book would be the result. I loved it."
—Jon Stewart

"Josh Lieb is one of the great brave journeys in American literature. Or maybe he just signed my name to a blurb he wrote. Either way, you have to admit he's brave. And the book is hilarious."
—Judd Apatow

"Josh Lieb has set literature back a hundred years."
—Daniel Pinkwater

"Beware, kids: Once your parents pick it up, they won't be able to put it down. (Guilty as charged.)"
—*New York Post*

★ "Pitch perfect . . . Every kid who's ever felt put upon, misunderstood, and, let's admit it, infinitely superior to his or her peers will laugh out loud as they enter Oliver's hilarious secret world."
—BCCB, starred review

"Lieb's creative and twisted first novel gets a positive vote."
—*Kirkus Reviews*

"Walter Mitty for teenagers, especially those who do not fit in. They will become huge fans of this book."
—*VOYA*

"This is a book that kids will be talking about."
—*School Library Journal*

Ratscalibur
josh Lieb

Part One of The Chronicles of the Low Realm

iLLustrateð By tom Lintern

razОr
bill

An Imprint of Penguin Group (USA)

A division of Penguin Young Readers Group
Published by the Penguin Group
Penguin Group (USA) LLC
345 Hudson Street
New York, New York 10014

USA / Canada / UK / Ireland / Australia / New Zealand / India / South Africa / China

Penguin.com
A Penguin Random House Company

ISBN: 978-1-59514-242-9

Printed in the United States of America

1 3 5 7 9 10 8 6 4 2

This is a work of fiction. Names, characters, places, and incidents either are the product of the author's imagination or are used fictitiously, and any resemblance to actual persons, living or dead, businesses, companies, events, or locales is entirely coincidental.

For Gus and Charlotte, the little rats.

Ratscalibur dreams, Ratscalibur sleeps . . .
Till babies hunger, mothers weep.
Then will a hero sword up-take . . .
Ratscalibur sings! Ratscalibur wakes!

JOEY DIDN'T WANT to move to the city, but his mom got a really good job offer, so here they were. The apartment was pretty small—just a bedroom for Mom, a bedroom for Joey, and a living room with a little kitchen attached. Right now it was full of brown cardboard boxes, stuffed with everything they owned.

"Joey, get me a knife," said Mom. She was sitting on the floor ripping open boxes. She was looking for the coffee maker, but she hadn't marked what box it was in. Mom drank a lot of coffee, so this hunt for the coffee maker was getting pretty desperate.

Joey handed her a steak knife. They had already unpacked most of the kitchen. There was still a lot of work to do, but he got kind of scared when he thought about what he'd do when they were *done*.

He didn't know anyone here. That morning, when he was helping the movers carry boxes, he'd spotted some boys across the street. They didn't look like the boys from back home. One of them raised his arm and started to wave at Joey, but the other boy—the bigger boy—punched him on the shoulder, and he put his hand down. After that they just watched.

The city was big. The city was loud. The city was dirty. It was *hot*, too, but that's the way it was in August anywhere. But *hot* in the  city meant *smelly*. Every piece of dog poop or pile of garbage bags seemed to have a little cloud of stink around it. Their apartment was on the ground floor, which worried Joey. That made it easy for crooks to just climb in the window. Mom said the iron bars on the window would keep the bad guys out, but that didn't make Joey feel any better. They hadn't needed iron bars on their windows back home.

"Aaargh!" said Mom, as she threw handfuls of Joey's underwear out of a box. Mom had a big vocabulary, but she sounded a lot like a half-awake animal when she didn't get her coffee. All her words would turn into grunts and groans. "No coffee. Coffee maker hiding," she said, and she dug some wrinkled money out of her purse and sent Joey down the street to buy a cup at the store on the corner.

The man at the store was nice, but he didn't speak any English. Joey didn't speak any Spanish, so they didn't have anything to say after Joey got the coffee. Next year, in seventh grade, Joey would start taking foreign-language classes. It would probably be a good idea to take Spanish.

As he walked home, the sidewalk was crowded with people

who were in a hurry to go somewhere and other people who weren't in a hurry to go anywhere at all. Joey was bounced around among them, like a pinball. He almost spilled the coffee one time, when a skinny man in a business suit brushed past him. As he was steadying himself, Joey caught a glimpse of a pile of garbage behind one of the buildings on the block. It was just a big mound of empty bottles, plastic trash bags, and broken baby toys . . . but something underneath the pile *moved*.

Joey ran home the whole way, not caring if he spilled a little. "Mom, Mom!" he called, as he came through the door—and then stopped. Uncle Patrick was there!

He must've just walked in, because he and Mom were still hugging, even though Mom looked a little annoyed. Uncle Patrick let her go and turned to Joey. "Hey, honcho!" He gave Joey a huge hug of his own. Uncle Patrick was big, big, big. He had big hands, big shoulders, and a big, *big* belly. He didn't have a job exactly, but he spent a lot of time watching football games, drinking beer, and falling asleep on the couch. He was kind of like a big friendly dog, which made sense. Mom said Uncle Patrick got along better with animals than people, anyway. He was Joey's favorite person, besides Mom.

"How you liking life in the big city?" asked Uncle Patrick. Uncle Patrick had lived in the city for a long time, and being close to him was probably the best thing about moving here. Before Joey could answer—before he could say anything about the weird boys across the street, or the bars on the windows, or the thing that *moved* inside the garbage—Mom said, "Pretty cute of you to show up after we've done all the moving, Patrick."

Uncle Patrick smiled. He had very white teeth, which were very crooked and stuck out of his mouth like jack-o'-lantern teeth. He ran his hand through his hair—which was very, *very* black and stuck out in messy spikes that looked sharp and dangerous, but were really soft when you touched them. "Aw, you know how it is, Sis," he said. "I meant to come by earlier but something came up."

"Yeah," Mom said, "I know how it is." She smiled to show she wasn't mad. She couldn't stay mad at Uncle Patrick for very long. He was her little brother—even if he was twice as big as her. Mom pointed at a box Uncle Patrick had brought in, which was covered with a dirty towel. "What's that?"

"That," said Uncle Patrick, "is a present for Joey. Go ahead, honcho, unwrap it."

Joey "unwrapped" the box—which really meant just pulling the towel off it. It wasn't a box, really. It was a cage, like people keep hamsters in, with a wheel for the hamster to run on, and a water bottle for the hamster to drink from, and everything. But the thing sleeping in the wood shavings at the bottom of the cage wasn't a hamster. It was twice as long as any hamster, and it had a pointed snout and a long, hairless tail. And everywhere else it was covered with pure silvery-gray fur.

"That," Mom said, "is a rat."

"NO, IT'S A PET RAT," said Uncle Patrick. "What better companion could a newcomer to the city have than the ultimate city animal?" He slapped Joey on the back. "Rats are survivors, my man. You can learn a lot from them. Besides, the fur reminded me of you."

Joey had mostly boring brown hair—not cool black hair like Uncle Patrick or bright red hair like Mom—but he also had this weird gray streak that ran along the side of his head over his right ear, like a racing stripe on a car. The streak was the exact same color as the rat.

"Where did you get it?" said Mom.

"The pet store," said Uncle Patrick.

"Is it safe?" asked Mom. "Has it had its shots and everything?"

"Sure, it's safe," said Uncle Patrick. "Would they sell it if it wasn't safe?"

"Why isn't it moving?" asked Joey.

Uncle Patrick nudged the cage. The rat snored a little and rolled over on its side. "It's sleeping," said Uncle Patrick. "Rats sleep a lot." He plopped down on the couch and started slapping the cushions. "Hey, nice couch."

Joey didn't know how he felt about having a rat for a pet. But he knew his mom wasn't going to let him get anything bigger. The building wouldn't allow it. A rat was better than a goldfish, he guessed. Besides, it was a gift from Uncle Patrick.

"I love it," said Joey.

Uncle Patrick smiled. "I knew you would. What are you gonna call him?"

Mom said, "Might I suggest 'Patrick'?" But she was smiling, too, so it didn't seem mean. Joey looked at the rat. It was just sleeping there in the wood shavings, with its fangs hanging out of its mouth, but it looked kind of special. It didn't look like a *Patrick*. Joey figured he'd come up with a better name later, when the rat woke up.

By the time Joey was ready to go to bed, though, the rat still hadn't woken up. Joey put a slice of turkey in the cage, but the rat didn't even seem to notice. Was it sick? Uncle Patrick had said that rats sleep a lot, but this seemed like too much.

"You're going to like it here, Joey. You'll see," said Mom. Then she hugged him and kissed him and turned out the light, just like she did when she said goodnight to him back home.

But this wasn't like going to sleep back home. The room was weird, and smelled weird. Joey's bed was in the wrong corner. None of his posters were on the walls yet. He lay in bed, with his eyes wide open, looking at the strange shadows his half-unpacked boxes made on the ceiling.

But the weirdest part was all the *noise*. Joey was used to it being quiet when he went to sleep. Here, *nothing* was quiet. Mom had left the window open a crack, for the fresh air. Now Joey could hear everything outside. Women walking on the sidewalk in their high heels: *KIK-kuk-KIK-kuk-KIK-kuk*. Cars growling past, blasting music from their stereos: *BOOM-boom-BOOM-boom*. Horns *honking*. Cats *howling*. People *laughing*. There even seemed to be a little voice, saying over and over again, "*Boy. Boy. Boy . . .*"

Joey listened closely. There *was* a little voice. It was tiny, but it sounded old and smart, like a professor in a movie. And the words were very clear.

"*Boy. Boy. Help me.*"

It wasn't coming from outside, though. Joey looked around the room. The voice seemed to be coming from his bedside table. Joey listened closer. It was coming from the hamster cage on top of the table.

"*Yes, boy. Yes. Over here.*"

Joey froze with terror. The voice was *coming from the rat.*

JOEY GOT OUT of bed to take a better look. The rat was still lying in the same place, but its eyes were finally open. Joey had expected them to be little black eyes, like strawberry seeds, but they were milky-white. "You can talk," said Joey. It wasn't a question.

The rat breathed heavily. It sounded painful. "Yes, but not very much. I am gravely injured."

Joey's mind felt completely blank. He didn't know what to think. This couldn't be happening. So he said, "Rats can't talk."

The rat scowled. "That is a very rude thing to say to a talking rat." But then the rat stopped scowling. "It's not your fault, I suppose. You are very young and ignorant. As you grow older, you'll discover that a lot of things can do a lot of things you didn't think they could."

Joey didn't understand what that meant, but he didn't want to get the rat mad at him again. "Who—who are you?"

"Aaah," said the rat, closing his eyes, "that is a much better way to start a conversation. I am Gondorff the Gray." He said it like it was something to be proud of.

"Gondorff . . . ?"

"The Gray," finished Gondorff. "I am the greatest Ragician in the realm."

These were words, but they didn't make any sense to Joey. "What does a Ragician do?"

"Oh, the usual," said Gondorff. "Spells. Potions. Incantations. You know, *Ragic*."

"Oh," said Joey, "don't you mean *Magic*?"

Gondorff scowled again. "Man does Magic. Rats do Ragic. It's just common sense. But that's a subject for another time." He opened his eyes and stared at Joey. "And who might you be?"

"I'm Joey," said Joey.

"Well, young Joey," said Gondorff, "I have an urgent mission I must entrust to you. You must go to King Uther and let him know . . ." Here the rat paused before finishing, "let him know that I *have failed*."

"What—what did you fail at?"

"It is too long a story for now. I haven't the strength of body or heart to tell it. Just take Uther my message. He will know what to do."

The rat hadn't moved anything but his eyes and mouth for the entire conversation. For the first time, Joey realized how much pain Gondorff seemed to be in. He pushed the water bottle and turkey slice closer to Gondorff's mouth. The rat ate and drank gratefully.

"Not that it will do much good," said Gondorff. "My time is short. I was dropped from high in the air by a BlackClaw who was trying to kidnap me. I managed to bite one of his toes off, so the BlackClaw let go . . . but I am no longer young enough to fly."

"How did you end up at the pet shop?" asked Joey.

"What pet shop?" snorted Gondorff. "The fat man picked me up from where I'd fallen and stuffed me into a cage he found in the garbage."

Joey nodded. That sounded like the kind of thing Uncle Patrick would do.

"Enough talk," said Gondorff. "I am weak, but I should have enough strength for a simple transformation. Give me your finger."

"What?"

"Your finger. Let me see it, boy."

Puzzled, Joey pushed his finger through the bars of the cage, right in front of the rat's face. Gondorff stared at the finger for a long minute. "Ah," he said, "Ah, yes . . . I see. That will do just fine." He turned his eyes toward Joey. "Now, tell me, boy—and this is important—do you give me this finger willingly?"

"Um, sure," said Joey.

"Good," said Gondorff the Gray, and he bit Joey's finger as hard as he could.

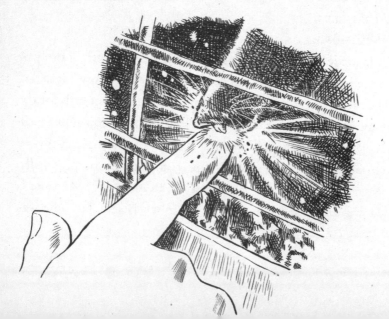

IT WAS THE WORST pain Joey had ever felt in his whole life, but it didn't even last a second. Before Joey could even yell or pull his finger away, the pain was gone. *Everything* was gone. For just a flash, the whole world went black, and Joey couldn't feel his finger or his legs or anything.

When the flash was over, Joey felt fine. He was on the floor, crouching on all fours, but he didn't hurt anywhere. He tried to stand up ... but it didn't seem to work right. He was able to stand, but he didn't get very high when he did. Just a few inches off the floor. The bedside table and the bed loomed high above him.

He looked at his hands, but they weren't his hands. They were little and pink, and they had sharp claws at the end of them. His arms were covered with brown fur.

"Oh no," said Joey.

He ran to the long mirror that hung on his closet door. But he didn't really *run*, he *scurried*—on his hands and his feet, because that felt more comfortable. And when he got to the mirror and stood up so he could peer into it, he knew what he would see peering back:

A rat's snout.

It was a little brown rat, about half the size of Gondorff. It had black eyes like baby watermelon seeds and a gray streak running down its right side, like a racing stripe. It had long silvery whiskers and a skinny bald tail. *And it was Joey.*

Joey felt his little rat face with his little rat paws. Yes, yes . . . that was him. He knew he should be scared—he was a rat. But he wasn't scared. Or maybe he was a little scared, but not nearly as scared as he would've thought he'd be.

"So, I'm a rat," he thought. "This is definitely the weirdest day of my life."

He looked at his rat feet: they looked a lot like his rat hands. He ran his "fingers" through his brown fur. It felt rough. He waved his tail back and forth and curled it around his body. That was fun. It was kind of nice to have a tail.

But just because he wasn't scared, it didn't mean he wanted to be a rat for very long. He scurried back to the bedside table. "Gondorff!" he squeaked. "Gondorff the Gray!" No answer. If the Ragician could hear him, he wasn't saying anything.

Joey jumped onto the side of his blanket (he was surprised at how high he could jump) and climbed onto his bed (he was surprised at how well he could climb). Then he leaped onto the bedside table and looked into the cage.

Gondorff looked sick. Very sick. Changing Joey into a rat must have been a lot of work. His eyes were open, but he didn't seem to see

anything. And he was lying very still. Joey couldn't tell if Gondorff was even breathing or not.

"Gondorff," said Joey, "are you dead? Please don't be dead."

Gondorff didn't say anything. He didn't move at all. And suddenly Joey was scared. Very, very scared. What if he was stuck being a rat forever?

Joey thought as hard as he could. Gondorff had said that he was the "greatest Ragician in the realm." That meant there must be other Ragicians. Maybe one of *them* could change him back.

But where would he find the other Ragicians? Where would he find the other rats?

His little nose twitched . . . and suddenly, he could smell the scent of rats *everywhere*. Like a cloud of competing smells, coming from every possible direction—through the window, under the floorboards, inside the walls—all spelling *R-A-T* in capital letters.

Joey shook his head. He didn't need just *any* rat. He needed *Uther*.

His nose twitched again. And, just like that, he knew where he had to go. No, it wasn't that simple; he didn't know *where* he had to go, but he knew *how to get there*. He could smell it. All the other rat scents dropped away, except for one. It smelled a little cleaner than the others. And . . . *fragile*.

It was like there was an invisible fishing line leading from

his nose, across the bed, out the window . . . and after that, he didn't know. But he knew that if he followed it, at the very end he would find *King Uther*. And where there was Uther, he would find Ragicians. The ones who could turn him back.

Joey's nose had never seemed very useful to him before. But he had a feeling now that—as a rat—a nose might be the most valuable thing he owned.

He gave a sad look at his bedroom door. He could hear Uncle Patrick snoring out in the living room. . . . He must've fallen asleep on the couch. Joey didn't like the idea of leaving without saying goodbye to Mom, but he was pretty sure she'd completely freak out if a rat crawled into her bed and tried to kiss her on the cheek. Considering what she did to cockroaches that dared just to walk across her kitchen floor . . . well, Joey didn't even want to think about what she'd do to *him*.

So he was leaving Mom without saying goodbye for the first time ever. That was depressing. But it's not like he had a lot of choices. . . .

Anyway, the sooner he left, the sooner he'd be back.

So Joey ran across the bed, hopped onto the windowsill, and dived out the window.

THE STREET SHOULD have been scarier at night than it was in the daytime, but Joey actually felt more comfortable now. Maybe it was because there were fewer people, and the ones that were out didn't seem to be in any hurry to go anywhere. But mostly, *probably*, it was because he was a rat.

"Rats," thought Joey, "must like city streets."

What rats definitely liked, he discovered, were smells. A lot of things that would usually gross him out were suddenly . . . *interesting* to him now.

Someone had left a chicken bone on the street. That smelled wonderful. There was a squashed cockroach under the tire of a parked bicycle. Mmm . . . that smelled like perfume.

There was even a dog poop on the corner that smelled like—

But Joey made himself look away before he could finish that thought. He couldn't get distracted now. He had to follow his nose and find a Ragician who would turn him back into himself, immediately.

He followed the invisible string down the sidewalk. It was easy for him to stay hidden. The only light was the moon and the streetlamps, and Joey made sure to keep in the shadows. It was like he didn't need much light to see, anyway. Just his nose.

The trail ran around a corner, into an alley behind a building. And suddenly Joey smelled something that didn't smell very good at all. It was coming from the pile of garbage that had scared him when he was getting Mom's coffee. The garbage looked even scarier at night. It was only up to his knee when he was a person, but now it towered over him like a black mountain.

The wheels of a broken baby carriage stuck out of the top of the pile and creaked eerily as they turned in the wind.

But the worst part was definitely the *smell*. "If dog poop smells good to a rat," thought Joey, "*everything* should." But this didn't smell good at all. It smelled like someone had shoved spicy peppers up both of Joey's nostrils. It didn't just smell bad, it *hurt*.

Something about the smell made Joey think about the *something* he'd seen moving in the garbage, and he shivered. Then he remembered that he was now a rat. He was *exactly* the kind of thing that moved inside garbage piles. Getting freaked out by garbage and the animals that lived in it was pretty silly.

The garbage mountain filled up most of the alley, except for a path a few inches wide. No matter how bad it smelled, if Joey was going to follow his nose, he was either going to have to climb over it or walk right next to it. "Well," thought Joey, "I'll just hold my breath and run as fast as I can. It'll only take a few seconds."

It was a good plan, but not so easy to follow. First of all, he had to go back into the street to take a deep breath where it didn't smell awful. Then, when he went back around the corner and tried to sprint past the garbage mountain, for some reason he couldn't keep himself from slowing down as he got closer, even though he told his legs to *run*. His legs *really* didn't want to run toward the pile. And even though he wasn't breathing, he could *feel* the bad smell in the back of his mouth, burning its way down his throat, like he was swallowing a lit candle made out of chicken fat. But he *pushed* himself, past the mountain . . . slowly, slowly . . .

The candle was in his stomach now. He could feel his insides burning up and leaking out his ears in green smoke. But that was just his imagination. He was so close to the end now. A little farther down the path. A brick wall to the left of him, the oily black garbage mountain to his right, and nothing but clean moonlight up ahead . . .

That's when the orange arm reached out and grabbed him. It pulled Joey, through wet reeking garbage, into the middle of the pile.

There was no time to think, but Joey knew what was happening. He didn't know *how* he knew, but he knew. *This was a cat.*

The only thing he *felt* were its claws sticking into the soft flesh around his neck. The only thing he *saw* was its dirty yellow teeth, about to snap down on him. The only thing he *smelled* was *death.*

The cat was going to eat him.

And suddenly Joey knew the only thing he could do.

Before the cat could *chomp*, Joey turned his head, extended his glistening white fangs, and sank them into the cat's paw.

The cat tasted like hot rotten peanut butter, but the bite worked. The cat *yowled* like a ghost and let go of him. Joey swam through the pile of coffee grounds, newspapers, and wormy banana peels—

The cat's claws raked across Joey's back. He could feel his fur growing moist with blood. But the claws hadn't snagged him. Joey leaped out of the garbage, into the alley.

And the cat leaped out right after him. She was a huge orange tabby, with snot-covered whiskers and gnashing teeth. Her paws

were dirty and scabby, her claws were mean, jagged splinters. She had one bright green eye and one dead black eye. And they were both looking right at Joey.

Without thinking he jumped into a hole in the brick wall and scurried to the back. Would it be deep enough? Yes. There was another, deeper hole at the back, like a cement nest. Joey dropped into it gratefully and rolled himself into a ball.

Above him, an inch away, the cat's claws scratched desperately at the bricks. *Scrabble-scrabble-scrabble.* But she couldn't reach him.

After a long, long time, she hissed with frustration and pulled her arm out of the hole. Then he heard her slither back inside her garbage mountain, to wait for the next tiny thing that tried to get past her.

Joey had never been so scared in his whole life. His little rat-heart was beating like a tom-tom drum.

He'd never been this tired before, either. And before he knew it, before he could even think if it was really what he should be doing right now, he was asleep.

"WHERE IS HE?" Mom said.

"I don't understand it," said Uncle Patrick.

The apartment was a mess. Every box was emptied, every door was open, every blanket was torn off every bed. Every place an eleven-year-old boy could possibly hide had been searched. Joey was gone.

Mom had woken up first and tiptoed past Uncle Patrick (who was still snoring on the couch) to wake up Joey. But Joey wasn't in his bed . . . or *under* his bed . . . or in his closet. He couldn't have gotten through the bars on the window, and the chain-lock was still bolted on the front door, so he couldn't have gotten out that way, either.

But somehow, Joey was gone.

That's when Mom started to freak out. She shook Uncle Patrick awake and made him help her look. They didn't find anything, except for the coffee maker, which had been stuffed at the bottom of a box of books in Joey's bedroom.

"I shouldn't have brought him to this stupid city," said Mom. She kicked the coffee maker across the floor, and it banged against the wall.

"Don't blame yourself," said Uncle Patrick. "You took this job for Joey. Joey is going to do great here—"

"Then *where is he?*" said Mom. She sounded like she was going to cry, but Mom *never* cried.

Uncle Patrick hugged her and patted her back. Mom started breathing normally again. She stood up very straight and took a deep breath. She looked down at Joey's bedside table.

"The rat is dead," she said, and then, like it was part of the same sentence, "I'm going to call the police."

She went into the living room to get her phone. Uncle Patrick looked at the hamster cage. The rat definitely wasn't moving. Uncle Patrick tapped the bars, to see if he could wake it up.

JOEY LIKED running on rat feet. They were tougher than human feet, so the ground didn't hurt, but he could still feel all the little pebbles and puddles he was running through, which felt really cool.

He had been running ever since the sun came up. The invisible trail he was following had led him down three alleys, over two wooden fences, and under one garbage dumpster. He hoped he would reach King Uther soon. He was very hungry. And Mom was probably pretty worried.

He jumped off a roof and slid down a long rain gutter, like it was a playground slide, and when he came out, he was *there*. Something in his brain went *ding*, like the GPS on Mom's car when it reached a destination. But he would've probably figured it out anyway. Because of all the rats.

They were everywhere. There were rats pushing wheelbarrows, and there were rats rolling around, wrestling. There were rats standing behind the counters of little wooden "stores," like shacks made out of sticks, selling bread crumbs and dried bugs and other things. There were soldier rats marching around with feathers tucked behind their ears. There were mother rats licking their little pink rat babies. There were rats laughing and yelling and crying. It was a whole village of rats. None of them paid any attention to Joey.

The rat village was on a square piece of land where four big buildings came together but didn't quite meet. There were a few bits of brown grass on the ground, but mostly it was dirt. The rats were going in and out of holes that went under the walls. Joey figured those must be the rats' "houses." There was one great big hole in the middle of a stone wall at the far side of the village, with rocks piled in front of it like steps, and fat rat soldiers standing guard. He could feel the little fishing line in his nose tugging him to that door. That must be King Uther's palace.

Something else tingled in his nose. Something strangely familiar and mildly unpleasant. Joey looked around . . . and jumped back when he saw a cat walking past him. But the smell wasn't nearly as bad as the big orange cat. This cat was smaller and cleaner, and black and white. But the strangest part was the little white rat riding on top of it, like a knight or a cowboy riding a horse.

None of the other rats seemed to be scared of the cat. A few of them yelled greetings to the white rat: "Halloo, Parsifur! Back from questing?"

And the little rat (who wore a peanut shell on his head, like a helmet) said, "For a bit, for a bit," and giggled like he'd said something funny.

Joey's nose twitched again. He smelled food, and he remembered how hungry he was. In front of each rat hole, the rats had laid out a little cloth, like a tiny picnic blanket. Now they were bringing food out of the holes and piling it in the middle of the blankets. It wasn't stuff he would've called food yesterday—a dirty raisin, a wilted piece of lettuce, a piece of beef jerky with little white worms crawling in it—but it sure looked good now. Maybe if the rats were having a picnic, they would share.

He looked around for something he could eat right away, without asking. In front of the king's palace, someone had left a big biscuit, just lying out there. There was a white plastic spork with a broken handle sticking out of the top of the biscuit. Joey thought that was weird. Who eats a biscuit with a spork? But it didn't look like anyone was trying to eat it now. Maybe he could have a nibble?

His nose answered him: *no*. With one sniff, all the way across the square, he could tell that the biscuit was too stale to eat, hard as a rock. Too hard for even his razor sharp teeth to gnaw at. This wonderful nose was more talented than he'd thought.

A giant fluffy brown rat with long, silky hair that trailed in the dirt was walking past the biscuit. This rat was tremendous, twice as tall as any of the others, and three times as round. It was *fat*. Its hair was so long you couldn't see its feet, so it looked like it was floating just above the ground, like a furry balloon. Joey didn't understand what he was looking at until he realized that it wasn't a rat at all—it was a guinea pig.

The guards in front of the palace started laughing when they saw the guinea pig. "Here to have another try, Brutilda?" But Brutilda—if that was her name—just ignored them and shook her woolly head as she passed. Joey noticed there was a ragged pink bow pinned to one of her ears.

"You dare show your face here, varlet?" someone said, surprisingly close to Joey. Joey looked behind him and saw a black rat on top of a gray cat. The rat had a lean and mean face, with scars all over it, like he did a lot of fighting. Luckily, he wasn't talking to Joey. He was yelling across the square, at the white rat Joey had seen before, who was still riding the black-and-white cat.

Everyone in the village hushed and watched. The white rat laughed with a brave squeak—*hee-hee-heeeeee*—and pushed the peanut shell to the back of his head. "Yes, I dare show my face, Drattleby." He gave a very big smile. His teeth flashed in the sun like little knives. "And why shouldn't I show my face? 'Tis a far more pleasant face than yours."

"Rogue!" hissed the black rat. He pulled a popsicle stick off the back of his cat, held it straight out in front of him, and dug his rat heels into the side of his cat. "Ya!" he yelled, "Ya!" And his cat started galloping straight at the white rat.

But the white rat wasn't scared. If anything, his smile got bigger. He pushed his peanut shell down over his face, pulled his own Popsicle stick out, and started galloping, right at his enemy.

And as he charged, Joey could hear him laughing behind his mask: *hee-hee-hee-heeeeee!*

And then they struck.

TWANG!

It was over in a flash. One second, the two rats were charging at each other as fast as they could. The next, the black rat was lying on his back in the dust. The white rat was still on top of his cat, and he was pointing his Popsicle stick down so it brushed at the fallen rat's neck. "I yield! I yield!" yelled the black rat.

At first Joey thought the black rat was bleeding, but then he saw that the Popsicle stick was just stained red at the tip with old Popsicle juice. The white rat didn't move. "Yielding won't be enough this time, Drattleby. I demand more."

The black rat hissed. "Curse you, Parsifur. What would you have of me?"

Parsifur, the white rat, smiled again. "You must tell me how pretty I am."

Drattleby made a lot of mean noises, but the white rat insisted, and after a few minutes of resistance, the black rat finally said, "You, Sir Parsifur, are the prettiest rat in the entire Low Realm."

"Besides King Uther, of course," said Parsifur. "But really, Drattleby, you're too kind." Then Parsifur let Drattleby get back on his feet, and everyone in the village stopped watching and went back to what they were doing before.

Joey thought that maybe he should ask this Parsifur to take him to see the king. He was a knight and everything, after all. But the white rat was already riding over to the far side of the village. Besides, Joey was hungry *right now*. Maybe he should have a little snack before he delivered his message to the king and got changed back into himself.

Joey edged over toward the nearest picnic blanket. Half a cucumber, a lemon peel, and some jelly beans were piled in the middle. Nobody was paying any attention to Joey, but he felt too scared to just *take* a jelly bean like he wanted to. Would he get arrested? Would the rats attack him for stealing?

Then he got lucky. The light in the village started to darken a little, and all the rats started scurrying into their holes. None of them said anything. They just looked at the sky and started going inside. As it got darker—and it got dark *fast*—more of the rats disappeared. Even the knights led their cats into a little alley where two of the walls came together. Joey guessed this was their stable.

Were the rats scared of a little rain? Joey looked up and saw a dark cloud hanging low in the sky, covering up the sun. A cold wind was starting to blow straight *down* on him in weird, regular beats: *whoosh-whoosh-whoosh*.

Almost all the rats were inside now, but Joey was way too hungry to be worried about a stupid thunderstorm, even if it had popped up awfully fast. Joey got right next to his intended target, a green jelly bean. Someone had bitten into it and spit it out, and there were some flecks of what was probably mayonnaise stuck to it, but it looked impossibly delicious to Joey. As soon as the last rats were inside—a few of the palace guards lingered at the doorway, looking up—he would grab his jelly bean, run to a corner, and feast.

It suddenly got *very* dark. The guards squeaked and jumped inside. The wind was really blowing down on Joey hard—*WHOOSH-WHOOSH-WHOOSH*—but all he could think about was that bright green jelly bean. He was reaching down for it. . . . It was finally his—

A skinny arm grabbed him by the leg and *yanked* him into the nearest hole, so that his claws only scratched at the surface of the candy. Somebody hissed, "Young fool!" Before Joey could even complain, he was inside the hole looking out—and seeing what had made the sky so dark, what had made the wind blow *down*. It wasn't a cloud: it was a huge flock of oily black birds. Crows. They covered every inch of the square.

Somebody tugged on Joey's back leg. "You trying to get yourself killed?" But Joey didn't answer or look back. His eyes were fixed on the crows. Especially one that had landed where he'd been standing, and who was now pecking at the hole Joey had disappeared into, as if the bird was still hoping to get an extra snack.

The crow had blank black eyes, like a doll. But it also had a long, sharp beak, like a shark's tooth. But the worst things were its claws. They were spindly and thin and mean. They raked up the ground like they were tearing open a little animal.

Joey gasped. *BlackClaws.*

AS QUICKLY as the invasion had begun, it was over. The crows each picked up a blanket by the corners, then folded the blankets over so that the food was wrapped up tightly. Then they flew back up into the air, clutching their bundles in their black claws.

It was suddenly bright and sunny in the village again, but none of the rats was in any hurry to go back outside.

Somebody slapped Joey on the ear. "Little dunce! What were you thinking?" Joey finally turned to see who had saved him. It was a pale gray rat mother, with a whole cave full of pink baby rats peeking out from behind her—and a few stuck to her chest, drinking. She was very skinny but very strong. Joey could see the webbing of her lean rat muscles rippling right beneath her fur. She wore an

orange Starburst wrapper around her head, like a handkerchief. And she was furious.

"I . . . I was hungry," Joey stammered.

"So you thought you'd take a snack from the *Tribute?*" she squeaked. "Young dung-for-brains. Here." She stuffed an acorn into Joey's paws and pushed him out of the hole. "Never darken my den again."

The village was starting to fill up again. Joey stood outside the hole, munching on the acorn, which tasted better than he thought it would. He could still hear the rat mother muttering to herself inside: "Nearly got myself killed for that half-wit. Never again. *Never!*"

Tributes. BlackClaws. Rat knights mounted on cats. It was all too much, too fast. Joey couldn't understand any of it. He figured the best thing to do was to deliver his message to the king and get changed back, as quickly as possible.

But when he climbed the steps to the palace, the guards wouldn't let him pass. "And where do you think you're going?" said the biggest one.

"I have a message for King Uther," said Joey.

The guards laughed. They stood on their hind legs and peered down at him, with their big bellies sticking out. Except for the fur and the teeth, they reminded Joey a lot of some of the bullies at his old school. "Nobody sees the king without an appointment," said the lead guard.

"But this message is from—"

"*Nobody*," hissed the guard, and he patted a toothpick he wore strapped to his side with a rubber band. *That's his sword*, Joey realized. The guard seemed mean enough to actually use it. Joey hopped

off the steps fast. But he had no idea what he should do next.

Life in the village had gone back to normal. Anybody who just showed up now wouldn't have any idea that the crows had even been there. But Joey knew, and it made him take in his surroundings with new eyes. Now he noticed that almost *all* the rats wore a weapon of some kind. There were swords made from toothpicks, and swords made from sharpened matches, and swords made from straightened-out paperclips. There were even some of those plastic swords that his mom put cocktail wienies on for Super Bowl parties. They looked more like real swords than some of the others, but Joey suspected that they probably weren't as strong.

Joey looked up at the sky and shivered. It made sense that everyone here had a weapon. He suddenly felt very helpless and naked. He was very aware of how soft his rat body was.

He looked around for something he could use to protect himself. A stick, a splinter . . . *anything*. But everything seemed to be taken.

And then he saw it. Right in front of his eyes, the whole time. The broken spork sticking out of the stale biscuit. Sure, it didn't look as useful as some of the other swords—the ones made out of paper clips looked especially dangerous—but it was *something* he could use, if he was ever attacked again. And maybe the guards wouldn't be such bullies if Joey had a sword of his own. Joey looked around to make sure the spork didn't belong to anyone. All the rats just walked past it like it wasn't even there.

Nobody paid any attention to Joey as he walked to the biscuit and scrambled up on top of it. It was definitely stale. The biscuit felt as cold and hard as the marble floor of a bank lobby. He could hear the guards behind him laughing about some mean joke, but he ignored them. He grabbed the broken handle of the spork and was surprised at how warm it felt. Like it was heated from the inside. He took his hands off, wiped them on his fur, and grabbed it again. Nope, still warm. Weird. Then he gave a good, hard tug. The spork stuck for a second . . . then came out of the biscuit with a kind of sigh, leaving four little holes where it had been. Joey weighed the spork in his hands, then tossed it from side to side. It was heavier than he'd expected, but it felt good. Useful. Joey felt like he could do some damage with it, if he had to.

Okay, so he had a weapon, now all he needed was a rubber band or a piece of string to tie it to his waist. He looked around to find one. . . .

He hadn't noticed how quiet the village had gotten. The guards had stopped laughing, the wheelbarrows had stopped turning, *everyone* had stopped talking. They were all staring up at Joey now, where he stood on top of the biscuit, holding his spork. Some of them were scared. Some of them were smiling. But all of them looked amazed. And no one said anything . . . until an old lady rat limped forward and pointed at him with a twisted paw: "The Spork in the Scone!" she shrieked, in a high, quavering voice. "He's drawn the Spork from the Scone!"

And then all the rats were yelling, "*The Spork in the Scone! The Spork in the Scone! Look! The lad has it! The Spork in the Scone!*"

The crowd surged forward. And suddenly a hundred little rat paws were grabbing at Joey, and a hundred little rat throats were screaming: "*Ratscalibur! Ratscalibur!*"

EVERYTHING HAPPENED very quickly after that.

The crowd picked Joey up and carried him in their paws to the palace. "Hey, wait!" yelled Joey. "I'll put it back! I'll put it back!" No one listened. They carried him up the steps and through the palace doors, past the guards (who looked kind of scared), and down long, long curving tunnels that were lit with flickering lamps. The walls were all covered with paintings of brave rats killing monsters. At the end of the longest tunnel, Joey was dumped on the ground, in a great big room filled with torches. Ancient tapestries hung from the walls, showing more brave rats defeating more horrible monsters and giant cats and hordes of terrible-looking wild rats. But the tapestries were faded and old, and there were big moth holes eaten through some of the heroes' faces.

A very old rat sat in a very large chair at the front of the room. He looked like he was sleeping with his eyes open, and then he woke up and seemed very surprised to be invaded this way.

This was like a nightmare. Trapped deep beneath the ground, with a crowd of rats at his back and some sort of half-dead rat zombie in front of him. Joey quivered in the dirt and wondered—honestly wondered—if he should just curl up into a ball and let them destroy him. But then he thought of Mom. He couldn't bear the thought of never seeing her again, or of leaving her wondering, forever, what had happened to him. Without even saying goodbye. So he forced himself to stand.

That's when he noticed that the old rat in the big chair wore some twisted tinfoil on his head. And that over his shoulders he wore a purple velvet cape, with the words CROWN ROYAL stitched in gold cursive across the bottom.

And the invisible fishing line from Joey's nose just seemed to *end* at the old rat's feet. . . .

Joey suddenly knew where he was. *This is the throne room*, he thought. *That's King Uther.*

Just as suddenly as the crowd had come in, they were gone. Joey was alone with the king. Except he wasn't. Joey saw that there were some other rats gathered around the throne that he hadn't noticed before.

There was a tall, strong-looking rat, with brown, gray-flecked fur, who stood protectively on the right side of the king.

There was a white rat, about Joey's size, with a bright pink nose and even brighter pink eyes. *She's pretty*, thought Joey, and then he added—very quickly—*for a rat*.

Brutilda the guinea pig was sitting in the corner, lumpishly, staring at Joey with hate. She had pulled her ear to her mouth and was chewing sloppily on her pink bow.

The tall rat stepped forward and held out a paw. "May I?" he asked. It took Joey a second to realize that he wanted to hold the spork. Joey handed it to him. The rat held it carefully and said, "Remarkable . . ." almost to himself.

"Who are you?" asked the pretty white rat.

"Joey."

She sat silent for a second. "That is a strange name for a hero."

"I'm not a hero," said Joey. "I'm just a boy who . . . okay, it's a long story. Who are *you*?"

She seemed very surprised by that. "Why, I am Yislene, Princess of the Low Realm, heir to the throne of Uther, and apprentice to Gondorff the Gray."

"Gondorff!" said Joey. "I know him! He—"

"Don't try to tell *us* about Gondorff, stranger," huffed the guinea pig with open hostility. "I've never heard him mention *you*."

"Brutilda, *please*," protested the tall rat, smoothly. "The stripling is our guest." He turned to Joey. "Allow me to introduce myself. I'm Sir Aramis, the king's vizier." He handed back the spork. Joey wasn't sure what a vizier was, but it seemed to be important. "And over there, always at the ready, is stout Brutilda, King Uther's loyal but occasionally short-tempered bodyguard."

Brutilda snuffled unhappily and glared at Joey.

Joey noticed that the king wasn't saying anything. In fact, it looked like he had gone to sleep again, though his eyes were still wide open.

"I really do know Gondorff," said Joey. "I have a message from him."

The room grew still. It was like everyone was holding their breath at once. The princess said, "Well, what's the message? Out with it!"

Joey swallowed. "The message is . . . that he has failed."

The vizier loomed closer. "He has failed? He has *failed*? Surely there's more to the message than that."

"No," said Joey, shrinking back. "He said King Uther would understand—"

"He said the king would *understand*?" squeaked Princess Yislene. "But we need to know more! When is Gondorff getting here? When will he explain himself personally?"

Joey swallowed again. It was like he had a tennis ball in his throat. He had a feeling this news was not going to go over well. Joey said, "He *won't* be coming here. I think . . ." he swallowed again, "I think Gondorff is dead."

The silence in the room was complete. Everyone had not only stopped breathing—it was like their hearts had stopped beating, too. Like their brains had stopped *thinking*. It was like a room full of statues was staring at Joey. Nothing. No sound. No breath. And then the spell was broken by a strange, ghostly voice chanting, "All is lost. *All is lost.* ALL IS LOST. *ALL IS LOST.*" Over and over, louder and louder.

It was the worst voice in the world. And Joey saw that it was coming from the waxy, slack-jawed mouth of the king.

YISLENE RAN TO her father to comfort him. She patted his arm and whispered soothing words into his ear, until he stopped moaning. Joey noticed that one of the king's legs was bent and broken looking, like something awful had happened to it and it had never healed right. It looked painful.

Once the king had been quieted, Sir Aramis asked Joey to tell his story, from the beginning. When Joey described how motionless Gondorff had been when he left him, the king moaned a little. When Joey told how he had escaped the orange cat in the trash pile (and showed them the scratches on his back), the princess gasped and said, "He escaped Wrundel. He was in Wrundel's den!"

"What's that?" said the vizier.

"Surely you've heard of Wrundel. She's the terror of the border to the eastern wildlands."

"I have more important matters on my mind," answered the vizier, who turned back to Joey. "Please continue."

Then Joey told about arriving in the village, the jelly bean, the spork . . . everything. When he was done, the vizier nodded sadly and said, "Well, there is little to do now but to submit to Salaman. His deadline for complete capitulation is tomorrow at midnight. Otherwise the BlackClaws will destroy Ravalon completely. We will have to do whatever he asks. . . ."

"What do you mean?" said the princess, waving a paw at Joey. "He has drawn Ratscalibur. We have our hero!"

"Princess, please," protested Sir Aramis. "You saw the note. We must declare ourselves under Salaman's command, or his BlackClaws will destroy Ravalon stone by stone!"

"But we have *our hero!*"

"I don't know what you're talking about!" said Joey. "I've delivered the message. Please, just turn me back into myself."

"Some hero," said Brutilda. She had a low voice, but it was very musical, like she kind of sang everything she said. That somehow made it scarier. She rolled toward Joey like a big hairy slug. "Look at him. He's no hero. Just a scrawny jumped-up High-Realmer with his hand on a power he cannot begin to understand. Come, little boy, and give Ratscalibur to someone who knows how to use it."

Joey didn't like being called little boy, but he held out the spork to her anyway. "Here, take it."

"No," said the princess, coming between them. "Brutilda, you have tried to take this sword countless times. It would not go to you—"

"I loosened it for him," protested the guinea pig.

43

"No," repeated the princess. "Your pure strength had no effect on it. You know that." Brutilda lowered her head. The princess continued, "This boy has something else in him. What it is, I cannot say. But Ratscalibur has chosen him. He is our hero."

Sir Aramis gave Joey a long look. He seemed to soften a little. As if a thought had occurred to him. *Maybe.* "I hope you're right. But it is a doubtful thing. . . . Only Squirrelin can confirm if this boy truly fulfills the prophecy. Or if the prophecy is a prophecy at all."

"Then he must go to Squirrelin," said Yislene, stubbornly. "That's who Gondorff was trying to see anyway."

Joey had had enough. "I don't know what you're talking about," he said. "Stop telling me about prophecies or whatever. Seriously. I'm not a hero. I'm just a kid. A *human* kid. And I need somebody to turn me back."

The princess and Sir Aramis shared a look, and the princess shook her head. "Gondorff never taught me the art of Transformation. And all the other Ragicians have fled this court."

Joey felt his blood run ice cold. "Then I'm stuck forever. As a *rat*? Isn't there anyone who can change me back into a person?"

Yislene frowned. "That brings us right back around to Squirrelin."

"Squirrelin," repeated Joey.

"Yes. Squirrelin the Squagician."

"Let me guess," said Joey. "He's a squirrel. Who does 'Squagic.'"

"Well, *obviously*," said Sir Aramis. "Now, what I'd like to know is—" but he didn't finish his question. He stopped and stared at something that had entered the room behind Joey. Before Joey could turn around to see it, he could *feel* it: a spicy scent tickling its fingers up his nose. A hot wind blowing on his back. And . . . something was *hugging* him. Wrapping itself around him and *squeezing.* Something very hot and very wet and *very* scratchy and—Joey looked down as it curled around his waist—very *pink*.

"*Hee-hee-hee,*" someone giggled.

Joey turned. The white rat, Sir Parsifur, had entered. Which would not have been very interesting, except he was still riding his cat, which had somehow shoved her head and shoulders into the throne room. She seemed determined to give Joey an all-over bath. "Be flattered, young one!" said the knight, leaping down. "Chequers likes you! "

The cat purred and licked Joey's snout.

"Parsifur!" yelled Aramis. "How many times must I tell you: that beast doesn't belong in the palace!"

"I couldn't agree more, Sir Stick-in-the-Mud. But, until I find a place more worthy of her perfection, it will just have to do."

The cat's tongue was now hugging all of Joey, slipping and squeezing around his whole body. He felt like he was the meat inside a burrito that was wrapped in a wet wool blanket instead of a tortilla. "M-make her stop," pleaded Joey.

Parsifur rapped the cat on the nose. "Cease, Chequers, cease! Our young savior has had enough."

The tongue retreated but not completely; it still tickled at Joey's belly.

"Checky! Behave!" bellowed Parsifur, twisting the disobedient cat's ear.

Chequers made an unhappy sound and pulled her tongue back into her mouth. Sir Parsifur made an apologetic face at Joey. "I really don't understand it. She's never acted that way before. You must taste uncommonly good." Parsifur gave Joey's shoulder a quick lick but seemed unimpressed. "Eh. Personally, I don't get it."

The knight drew his sword and bowed grandly before Joey. "Allow me to formally introduce myself. I am Parsifur. Known to my enemies as Parsifur the Vain. Known to my friends . . . as Parsifur the Vain." He winked. "I'm really very vain."

"Better known as the Giggling Knight," put in Brutilda, who didn't seem to like Parsifur any more than she liked Joey.

"Possibly, large one, possibly," replied Parsifur, "Though I wouldn't know why." Then he giggled: *hee-hee-hee.*

The princess looked at him impatiently. "We're in the middle of some very important business, Pars. . . ."

"Oh, I know," said the knight. "Which is why I have come to offer this young stripling my services." He knelt before Joey. "I am yours to command."

Joey felt even more scared than he had when the cat had been licking him. "Wh-what do I need your services for?"

Parsifur gave a big, friendly smile. "Why, for your quest, of course."

PARSIFUR TOOK A giant swallow of golden liquid out of a cup made from an acorn cap. "Stop this nonsense. Of *course* you're going on a quest."

They were sitting in a long drinking hall. It had a very low ceiling and very long tables, and the chimney for the fireplace didn't seem to work, because the whole room was full of smoke.

It was also full of rats. Big rats, tiny rats, fat rats, skinny rats. Rats with no teeth, and rats with no hind legs. Rats with too much fur, which sprouted out of their ears and down the middle of their backs like hair fountains. These were tough rats, and they had all been drinking and fighting and yelling a few minutes ago. But everyone had gone instantly silent as soon as Joey and Parsifur walked in.

Parsifur hadn't been silent at all. He'd grabbed his cap full of golden liquid from a passing barmaid and loudly demanded a bowl of stew for Joey.

Joey had never felt more out of place in his life. "Doesn't it bother you that everyone is watching us?"

Parsifur shrugged. "I'm used to everyone watching me." He burped and giggled—*hee-hee-hee*.

A very plump young barmaid approached and put a bowl of stew, freshly scooped from the pot over the fire, on the table in front of Joey. The bowl shook in her hand. She stared at Ratscalibur, which lay on the bench next to Joey, like it might jump up and bite her.

"Thank y—" said Joey, but before he finished she shrieked and ran away. Joey was too hungry to care. He stuck his snout into the bowl and didn't make any noises but eating sounds for several minutes. The stew tasted . . . *incredible*. After a while, he turned his gravy-stained nose up to Parsifur and asked, "What am I eating, by the way?"

Parsifur had a funny smile on his face. "You plan to become human again, correct?"

"As soon as possible!" said Joey.

Parsifur's smile widened. "Then I won't tell you what's in the stew. It might be an unpleasant memory later."

Joey thought about that for just a second, then dived back into the stew.

Parsifur let Joey eat in silence, but as soon as Joey started licking the bottom of the bowl, he said, "Now, to resume. Of *course* you're going on a quest, just as soon as the stablehands finish getting our cats and saddlebags ready. It's the only way to save Ravalon. And the only way you'll ever get back home."

"What's Ravalon?"

"Where you are now. Uther's kingdom. There's Bragadoon to the north, Peacemeal and Belle Garden to the south, Gronkonkomo to the east—and a million more besides. But Ravalon, fair Ravalon . . . this was the brightest pearl of the Low Realm. But now there is Salaman. . . ." Parsifur took another swig of the golden stuff. "And all our friends to the north, south, and east have abandoned us."

"Salaman is another kingdom?"

Parsifur shook his head. "Salaman is a Ragician. No one had ever heard of him until a year ago, when his BlackClaws first arrived. They brought a note from him, demanding a weekly tribute, or he would destroy Ravalon. Some of us wanted to fight back, but BlackClaws are strong, and the king is . . . not himself. The vizier thought it best to give tribute and hope that things would get better." Parsifur giggled. "Things have not gotten better. They rarely do, do they?" He giggled even harder.

"Now, all the strongest knights and Ragicians have fled Ravalon. And all we are left with is those who are too damaged"— he gestured to the battle-scarred rats around him—"or too loyal"—and he tapped himself on the chest—"to leave."

Joey saw Drattleby, the rat Parsifur had jousted with, glaring at them from across the room. *Which kind is he?* wondered Joey. *Damaged or loyal?*

Joey didn't see what any of this had to do with him. "Why don't you just go . . . *fight* Salami-man—"

"Salaman," corrected Parsifur.

"Whatever. You're a knight, right?"

"Am I? Sometimes I wonder," said Parsifur. "Anyway, I don't know where to find Salaman. Nobody's ever even *seen* him. There are rumors, of course . . . that he's a giant rat, midnight-black, fangs like spearheads. Real bogeyman stuff. All we know for sure is that he's immensely powerful. Controlling BlackClaws is no easy thing. Their brains are so small, only the most cunning -agic can ensnare them." He waved his empty cup at the barmaid. "Bring me another, love.

"That's why Gondorff went to seek help from Squirrelin. Gondorff was strong, but Squirrelin is even stronger—he was Gondorff's *teacher.* The old fellow's saved Ravalon more than a few times in the past."

Joey said, "So Squirrelin's like this super-good guy?"

Parsifur's smile stretched so wide it covered his entire white muzzle. "Squirrelin is *awful.* Tiny. Mean. Secretive. Greedy. But you can't hold that against him. He's a squirrel. And Squagic is a harsh tonic. It always brings out the worst in them." A rat eavesdropping nearby nodded. "Squirrelin is the most powerful worker of -agic ever known, so it's understandable that the Squagic has had some . . . less than positive effects on his personality. He keeps to himself, far from the wars, diseases, and *emotions* that plague us lesser creatures. But Aramis thought that if anyone could get Squirrelin to help us, it would be Gondorff. He was our last hope." Parsifur paused for a second. "I think you know how that ended."

Joey looked at his pink rat claws. He knew *exactly* how that ended.

"But then . . . a new hope. A stranger appears from nowhere and plucks Ratscalibur from her petrified scone, where she's rested these many years, ever since Uther's great-grandfather Axel Stone-Heart stuck her there. And this stranger, perhaps, will fulfill the prophecy. . . ."

"What prophecy?"

"A poem we say around here. No one's sure where it came from. Nurses sing it to babies in their cradles. Some think that's all it is, just a nursery rhyme. It goes on for a while, but the part that's pertinent to you goes . . ." And here Parsifur took a deep breath, closed his eyes, and recited in a high-pitched sing-song tone:

Ravalon thrives, Ravalon bustles
Mercy and beauty and wisdom and muscle.
And old Axel's spork slumbers stuck in the scone,
Unneeded by rat kings on Ravalon's throne.

But as seasons change, so must Ravalon, too.
All good times must end. The reckoning's due.
Ratscalibur rests whilst Ravalon turns
Crops drop to dust, Ravalon burns . . .

Ratscalibur dreams, Ratscalibur sleeps . . .
Till babies hunger, mothers weep.
Then will a hero sword up-take . . .
Ratscalibur sings! Ratscalibur wakes!

The little white rat paused, as if he hoped he could live in the poem a little while longer, then shook his head and opened his eyes. The entire room had listened to him recite. The only other sound was the soft snap of wood in the fireplace. Now everyone was staring at Joey again, just as intently as when he'd first walked in. Hundreds of eyes, wide-open, were shining blankly at him. It was almost too much to bear.

"So that look in their eyes," whispered Joey. "That's hope?"

Parsifur gestured toward the door with an elegant paw. "Maybe out there in the courtyard," he said. "But *these* eyes, in here . . . these are the eyes of soldiers who've fought and suffered and grown old on the battlefield. These eyes have seen blood and death and real heroism. No, that's not *hope* you see in *these* eyes," Parsifur giggled. *Hee-hee-hee.* "It's disappointment."

As if to punctuate the words, Drattleby suddenly stood up and yelled, "This . . . skinny *boy* is our *savior?!*" He sounded completely disgusted. He threw his cup to the floor with a *clatter* and stormed out.

Parsifur squeezed Joey's paw. "But you'll show them, won't you, lad?"

Joey didn't know what to say. He didn't want to show *anything* to *anybody.* He just wanted to go home. "Why are you telling me all this . . . terrible stuff?"

Parsifur stopped smiling for a second. "What kind of hero would you be if you didn't know what you were facing?"

Then Brutilda entered and stood in the doorway, breathing heavily: "The cats are ready."

JOEY AND PARSIFUR followed Brutilda out the door. A long line of cats stood in the courtyard, with water bottles and other provisions strapped to their sides. The cat in the middle was . . .

"Chequers!" squealed Parsifur. "Your tack is a mess." He rushed to tend to his black-and-white mount.

Joey stared at the cats. Was he actually expected to ride one of these beasts?

But he didn't get a chance to wonder long. A set of claws latched around his upper arm in an iron grip and *yanked*. Joey found himself being dragged across the courtyard by Brutilda, who wasn't even looking at him. "Wh-what are you doing?" Joey spluttered, but the giant didn't bother to answer. She dragged him through the dirt, past a guard (who didn't do a thing to help Joey), in through a little door at the side of the palace, and down an incredibly steep, dark staircase before Joey could even yell out "Help!"

Is this how it ends? thought Joey. *Murdered in a basement? By a guinea pig?*

At the bottom of the stairs, Brutilda shoved him through a gap in some thick cloth, and he found himself back in the throne room. He looked behind him, but the old tapestry he'd been pushed through had swung shut, and Brutilda hadn't followed.

Uther still sat on the throne, completely unmoved since the last time Joey had seen him. Hugging his legs and kneeling at his feet was his daughter, Princess Yislene. Her eyes were squeezed shut and she was whispering something. It seemed like a very private moment. Joey was sure he shouldn't be there, and he was just starting to wonder if Brutilda actually *would* murder him if he backed out through the tapestry, when Yislene opened her eyes and said, "Thank you for coming. Please step closer."

Reluctantly, Joey walked toward the princess and the king. He found himself staring at the old rat's vacant, unseeing face. *This is the great King Uther?* As if she could read his mind, Yislene said, "He wasn't always like this." Joey looked away from Uther, embarrassed. Yislene continued, "Until a few years ago, he was the strongest, wisest, bravest king in the Low Realm. The most respected, and the most feared, since Axel . . . or even Ajax. There are countless rats—and others—who owe him their lives. Just ask Brutilda."

Joey thought it was highly unlikely he would ever do that.

The princess continued. "But my mother died in an accident. . . . She fell down the great staircase in the southern tower. . . . And something changed in him after that. He didn't grow weak right away. He just lost some of his will. One day, two years ago, he was

wounded while helping Gronkonkomo repel invaders from the Savage River. Perhaps his grief had made him careless. Sir Aramis was by his side in battle and carried him home. We thought, with a little rest, his leg would heal. But instead it's become more twisted and poisoned than ever. And his mind has been poisoned along with it. But—" she said, and then repeated, emphatically, "*but* his spirit is not all gone. There are a few good days, mixed in with the many bad. King Uther is still in there."

She looked up at Joey, imploringly. "That's why we have to reach Squirrelin. That's why we have to defeat Salaman. I can't let anyone steal his kingdom while the true king, my father, lives!"

Joey nodded. He understood. It had been just him and Mom, as long as he could remember. Mostly Mom working—and *working*—to make sure Joey had enough to eat, and a bed to sleep in, and clothes to wear. Even taking this job in the city . . . Joey knew that she had done that for *him*. If anyone ever tried to hurt Mom . . . there wasn't anything Joey wouldn't do to protect her.

But he didn't understand why they needed *him*. "You're a Ragician," he said. "Why don't you just send, like, a psychic message to Squirrelin so he'll come and save the day?"

Yislene shook her head. "It doesn't work that way. You can't send complicated messages through Ragic. At most, you can say 'Come

55

now' or 'Stay away.'" And then, as if she could read Joey's mind again, she said quickly, "And if you think Squirrelin would come just because I said, 'Come now,' well, you don't know Squirrelin. He is a stalwart friend of Ravalon . . . but he takes some convincing to do *anything*."

There was a rustling behind Joey. Brutilda had entered through the tapestry. She nodded at the princess, who said, "We must leave. But there's one more thing you deserve to know." She hesitated, then said, "Considering all the cloaking spells Gondorff was traveling under, there's only one way the BlackClaws could have found him."

She hesitated again, so Brutilda finished the thought for her: "Salaman must have a spy in the king's court."

Joey's mind spun. "Wait," he said, "the bad guy *knows* we're coming? Why are we even trying then?"

The princess stood, kissed her father on the cheek, and turned to Joey. "Because we have no choice," she said, and then she walked through the tapestry with Brutilda.

Joey stood there, alone for a moment in the silent throne room. *Because we have no choice.* She was right. If he wanted to get back to Mom, if he wanted to become *Joey* again . . .

His thoughts were interrupted by a dry tickle on his wrist. He looked up to see that Uther had reached out to him with a feeble paw. A spark of . . . *something* was in the old man's wet eyes. Then he whispered, so softly that Joey wasn't sure he'd heard it, maybe he just *felt* it: "*Thank you.*"

Then the spark was out, and the king's eyes went cloudy again. Still, Joey mustered a "You're welcome, Your Majesty," before he turned to climb the stairs. His mind was fixated on one thought:

He had no choice.

JOEY HAD NEVER ridden a camel, but he bet it must be a lot like riding a cat. For every step the cat took forward, it felt like it was taking two steps up and two steps down. He'd ridden a horse one time at summer camp, but this was different. This made his little rat stomach do flip-flops.

"Oh, the *look* on your *face!*" giggled Parsifur, who was a little ahead, riding Chequers. "Don't tell me you're mount-sick! Yislene loaned you the smoothest cat in her stable."

Joey felt like throwing up, but he didn't want to give Parsifur the satisfaction. "I'll get used to it," he said. He scratched the back of his cat's head, so that the cat wouldn't think Joey blamed him. He was really a very nice cat: a big black tom named Squamish. But riding Squamish was like being strapped to a trampoline in an earthquake. And that's when he wasn't jumping from building to building.

They were traveling across rooftops now. Yislene led the way, riding her snow-white cat, Questel. Then Parsifur and Joey, with Aramis riding right behind Joey, and sour Brutilda—riding an enormous ginger cat named Bicker—bringing up the rear.

"I thought cats ate rats," said Joey.

"Normal cats do," said Parsifur. "But if you find a kitten and raise it . . ." He twisted Chequers's right ear. "Well, you'll find no more loyal comrade in the world."

"Do any cats talk?" asked Joey.

"I've never met one who could," Parsifur said. "But I think they probably would . . . if they ever found anything worth saying." He twisted Chequers's other ear. The lean cat grinned.

Talking to Parsifur was exhausting. Joey was never sure if the little knight actually meant what he was saying. Still, talking beat listening to himself *think*. "How long do we have to ride?"

"Not long," said Parsifur. "Hopefully no more than a day."

"A whole *day*?" Joey gasped. This thing seemed like it was going to stretch out forever. Poor Mom. . . .

"Possibly longer, depending on what we run into. Of course, we can't go longer than tomorrow night, or we won't have any kingdom to go home to." Parsifur looked at Joey's face and giggled again: *hee-hee-hee*. "You are positively the least heroic hero I've ever run across. It's really very amusing. But Squirrelin will know what to do with you."

"The only thing I want Squirrelin to do is turn me back into a person."

Parsifur kept smiling. "From what I've seen of people, I'd rather stay a rat."

Sir Aramis's cat, a sleek gray beast named Mave, pulled up alongside Joey and Squamish. Aramis leaned in to Joey. "You're still not convinced you are a hero?"

Joey put his hand on Ratscalibur, which was now tied securely to his side with a piece of dental floss. He wished it would make him feel brave or strong, but he didn't feel anything. The handle wasn't even warm anymore. "I *know* I'm not a hero," said Joey. "I'm sorry, but I'm not. I get picked last for kickball." Then he added, "You don't think I'm a hero either, do you?"

Sir Aramis sighed. "I would like to believe . . . but I am a practical rat. I have a hard time putting faith in a 'prophecy' that my sisters taught me while we were skipping rope."

They had come to the edge of another building, and Aramis called ahead to Yislene, "Princess! Halt! This is the western border."

The rats all jumped off their cats and looked around. Sir Aramis

stood at the edge of the roof. "Here, Ravalon ends, and the wild west begins. No kings hold sway in the land beyond. Just wild animals . . . obeying no law but their own hunger." He pointed to a wide green park about eight blocks away. Joey knew about that park. He and Mom were supposed to go visit it today. "There, in the middle of that bramble, you will find the lair of the Squagician." Joey took a deep breath. Instantly, his nose told him exactly where he needed to go.

The vizier turned to Yislene. "Princess, is there no way I can convince you to return with me and leave this quest to the others?"

Yislene shook her head stubbornly. "This quest is our last chance to survive. If it fails, our defeat will be final. We will have to submit to Salaman. Uther will step down. Ravalon will be no more. As the last Ragician in Uther's realm, it is my duty to aid and protect these adventurers as best I can."

Aramis looked like he wanted to say something more, but then he stopped, because he saw it would be hopeless. Joey could see that Aramis really *was* a practical rat.

"Well, then," said Sir Aramis, "I wish you luck on your journey. Now I must return to my place by the king—"

"Ow!" shouted Joey. Something was *burning* him in the side. He looked down, expecting to see that his fur was on fire, but the only thing there was Ratscalibur, glowing faintly . . . and then he felt a cold wind beat down on his head. *Whoosh—whoosh—WHOOSH—*

"Look out!" Joey yelled, just as the crow swooped down at them. The other rats dropped flat to the ground . . . except for Yislene, who stood frozen in place.

Joey was frozen, too, as he watched the crow snatch her up in its black claws and fly away.

15

THE CROW didn't fly far. With a yell, Sir Aramis leaped from the roof, grabbed hold of one of the bird's legs, and hacked at the other leg with his sword. The BlackClaw squawked and dropped Yislene onto the rooftop. It squawked again, bitterly—clearly annoyed at losing the princess—then grabbed hold of Sir Aramis before *he* could get away, too.

The BlackClaw flew high into the air clutching the vizier, who continued hammering away at it with his sword. Aramis was shouting at the bird, but whatever he was saying, they couldn't hear it on the roof.

The cats were up on their hind legs, leaping and hissing and stretching their paws out at the crow, pumping their limbs like

they were trying to swim *up* through the air to rescue Sir Aramis. But they couldn't even get close, and they kept falling helplessly to the roof: *thump-thump-thump.* . . . Only Aramis's own cat, Mave, remained still. She sat on her haunches and stared calmly up at the furious battle taking place above her head. She was probably the only cat smart enough to know that that was all she could do.

It was all Joey could do, either. He didn't know exactly what a vizier's job was . . . but he'd never imagined *this.* "Aye," said Parsifur, who was standing next to him. "Aramis was one of our bravest knights, till he decided his time was better spent holding the king's hand."

"How did you know what I was thinking?" said Joey.

Parsifur laughed, but he didn't sound happy. "It's no great chore to read your face." Then he continued as he stared up at the vizier. "Aramis taught me everything I know. I was his squire."

"You don't seem to get along now," said Joey.

Parsifur spat on the ground. "I'm of the opinion that a knight should *fight.* Not play politics in the king's court." He giggled, but

his eyes looked deadly serious as they stared up at Aramis. "But perhaps braver rats make better choices."

The battle raged on. Aramis kept jabbing the crow with his sword, but to no effect. Every few moments, the crow would try to fly higher into the air . . . but it kept bumping into something—something *invisible*, as far as Joey could see—and doing a weird little flip. "Why's it flying like that?" asked Joey.

Brutilda, solemnly gnawing on her broadsword, grunted, "The princess has it on a leash."

Joey looked at Yislene. She was waving her paws in front of her face and muttering something under her breath as she stared at the crow. Joey understood: this was Ragic. "Can't she do anything more?"

"She could stop the crow's heart," said Parsifur, "but a fall from this height, trapped in a BlackClaw's death grip, would be difficult to survive. If the fall didn't kill Aramis, the weight of the bird might."

"Or a talon might pierce his heart," said Brutilda.

"Aye," nodded Parsifur. "This is the wisest course. Eventually, the BlackClaw will grow frustrated and drop Sir Aramis"—this was the first time Joey had heard Parsifur call the vizier *Sir* Aramis. "All the princess can do is make sure he doesn't fall too far."

As if on cue, the crow gave up and opened its claws. Aramis fell soundlessly through the air, past the roof, to the street below. There was a little *thud* on the roof near Joey, but he was too worried about Aramis to wonder what it was. He ran to the edge of the roof and looked down.

To his relief, he saw that the vizier had fallen on what looked like a nice soft pile of trash in a narrow alley. He lay flat on his back, not moving, but even from here Joey could see that he was breathing. "Probably just stunned," said Parsifur, as he jumped onto Chequers. "I'll go down and fetch him."

The crow took one last look at the fallen knight, then flew away with a disgusted *squawk*. Joey glanced over at Yislene. She had collapsed with exhaustion—that was the *thud* Joey had heard—and Brutilda was trying to get her to sip water from an acorn cap.

Parsifur, riding Chequers, leaped onto the building's fire escape and started trotting down the steps. Joey looked down. Aramis had raised himself up on an elbow and was looking around, a little dazed. But he seemed to be okay. Joey was relieved.

Then Joey looked at the pile of garbage Aramis was lying on. It seemed familiar. He had definitely seen it before. Maybe not from this angle. He turned his head and squinted, just as a little tickle of hot spice ran its fingers up his nose. . . .

Something clicked in Joey's brain. "Wrundel," he whispered. "That's Wrundel's den." Then, suddenly he was shouting at the top of his lungs, "*Sir Aramis is on top of Wrundel's den!*"

He looked back down: Aramis was still dazed, absolutely helpless. The garbage bag he was lying on *rippled*, as if blown by a breeze no one could feel. Or as if something was *moving* beneath it . . .

"YA!" shouted Parsifur without a moment's hesitation, kicking Chequers's sides with his heels. The cat leaped off the fire escape obediently—falling a full three stories onto the garbage pile, right next to Aramis, and somersaulting forward. Only at that moment did Wrundel's savage orange arm stab out of the pile. But Parsifur, who'd been thrown by the fall, stabbed back with his trusty sharpened paper clip. Wrundel's paw disappeared into the pile with a scream. Before it could reappear, Parsifur had leaped back onto Chequers, pulled Aramis up behind him, and ridden away.

A few minutes later, Chequers, carrying the two rats, climbed back onto the roof. Both knights looked exhausted by the recent ordeal, but Sir Aramis had recovered his senses enough to speak. "I owe you my life, good Parsifur," said the vizier with dignity.

Parsifur gave a significant look to Yislene, who was now able to stand without Brutilda's help, and said, "We owe you far more than that."

Aramis waved the compliment away with a dismissive gesture, as if saving the life of a princess was something he did every day. "Your Majesty," he said, turning to Yislene, "in light of this recent ordeal . . . please reconsider going on this quest. I worry. Losing you would be the end of your father."

But the princess, though shaken, was as stubborn as ever. "Losing his *kingdom* would be the end of my father," she said. Aramis had to nod regretfully. She smiled and hugged him and gave him a grateful kiss on the cheek. "Don't worry, old fellow. My companions will keep me safe." Aramis didn't look too sure about that, but he hugged her back, then nodded stiffly to the others and mounted his cat, to return to his king. He trotted away, giving several worried glances back as he left.

The princess turned to the others. "Let us make haste. There is much riding to do today." The others mounted their cats and followed her down the fire escape, onto the street, around the corner from Wrundel. Parsifur leaned toward Joey and whispered, "We'll not ride far before we make camp. Ragic is exhausting—especially for one as young as Yislene. She'll need to sleep soon."

Joey nodded, though it was taking all his concentration to hold on to Squamish as she padded down the fire escape. He felt like he was riding a Slinky downstairs.

It was broad daylight, and there were plenty of people on the street, but no one paid any attention to the strange caravan winding down the sidewalk. "Why don't they see us?" asked Joey.

"It's the basic -agic," said Brutilda, as if he were an idiot. "*Everyone* knows that."

"Tut-tut, Your Roundness," said Parsifur, "the boy was a High-Realmer only yesterday. He can't be expected to know such things." Brutilda sniffed and looked away.

Parsifur said to Joey, "All those who work -agic, whether they be Ragicians, Squagicians, Dogicians, Raccoogicians—"

"That's . . . raccoon magicians?" said Joey.

Parsifur nodded. "They all have an interest in keeping our world—the Low Realm—hidden from yours. So, whatever else they do with their powers, there is a basic -agic that they do at all times, every second that they breathe, that clouds our realm from human eyes. High-Realmers can see individual pieces of the puzzle—a cat here, a rat there. But a rat riding a cat? Never. That's why Gondorff had to turn you into a rat to send his message. You never would have *seen* us, otherwise.

"And when they do stumble upon one of us, say after we've died in battle, what do they find? Nothing. Take me, for example. The human who chances to find my corpse will merely see a rat, a peanut shell, and a paper clip. Nothing suspicious there. Aside, of course, from my outstanding physical beauty. *Hee-hee-hee.*"

Joey realized it had been a long time since he'd heard Parsifur giggle. He was kind of glad to hear the noise. But something still didn't make sense. "Okay, but why are we traveling on the sidewalk at all? Shouldn't we be in the sewer? Wouldn't that be faster and safer? Isn't that where rats *live*?"

Brutilda, riding ahead of them, snorted. "There's nothing *safe* about the Under Realm. And the only thing it would make *faster* is our deaths." She spat a loogie onto the sidewalk.

"Allow me to translate what my ovoid friend has put so bluntly," said Parsifur. "The Under Realm—or 'sewer,' as you refer to it—is inhabited by wild rats. Savages who have never mastered cats or Ragic or weapons—"

"They have spears," interrupted Brutilda.

"—Except for the crude spears they throw, thank you, Brutilda," he said in a way that didn't sound like *thank you* at all. "They're content to lurk in the dark and steal whatever they can find and kill whomever they can meet. They have no leaders, no kings, no civilization, no honor. What they have are *numbers*. There are *lots* and *lots* of them. Any civilized animal that finds itself in the Under Realm doesn't last very long."

Joey shivered. He was suddenly very glad to be on the sidewalk, in bright sunlight. He just wished they could go faster. *Mom must be so worried.*

Brutilda suddenly took hold of the reins of Yislene's cat and brought it to a halt. She turned back to the others. "We must stop here for the night," she said, leaving no room for argument. "The princess must rest."

"Nonsense, Brutilda, I'm fine. . . ." said Yislene. But even Joey, who barely knew her, could see that she wasn't. She was leaning sideways in her saddle, like she could fall asleep any second.

They found a ventilation shaft—an aluminum tunnel full of hot air—beneath a pizza parlor and crawled inside, while the cats stayed outside and guarded the entrance. It was cozy and warm, and the air was filled with the luxurious smell of fresh pizza. It suddenly occurred to Joey that he was *starving*. "I didn't even realize how hungry I was," he said to Parsifur.

"Aye," said the knight, tightening his belt, "There's no diet like fear. But have no worries: we'll raid the establishment above us once it closes for the night."

Yislene was already asleep on a bed of cloth and straw that Brutilda had laid out for her. The giant guinea pig guarding the princess sat upright on her mammoth haunches. Joey felt sorry for anyone who tried to get past *her*.

Joey nudged Parsifur and pointed to Brutilda. "What's her story?" he whispered.

"I have ears," said Brutilda. Joey had forgotten how well rodents could hear.

"Take no offense, O bulbous one," giggled Parsifur. "The boy's curiosity is only natural. Fair Brutilda is an escapee from what you would call a . . ." he hesitated. "Now what is the term?"

"Kindergarten class," hissed Brutilda.

JOEY WAS CONFUSED. He had never heard the word *kinder-garten* spoken with such loathing.

"Yes, 'kidneygordon class,'" repeated Parsifur, saying it all wrong. "As I understand it, it is a place where immature humans are herded together until they can be of use to the adult colony."

"Well, it's something like that," said Joey.

"It was the fingers that got to me," said Brutilda. "All those filthy human children, pushing their rude fingers through the bars, poking at me, *prodding* me, day after day after *day*." Brutilda kept talking, but she didn't look at Joey or Parsifur. It was like she was lost in some unhappy memory inside her mind. "And the stuff that was *on* those fingers ... the dirt and the paint and the paste and the boogers ..." She stopped talking and licked her mouth for a long

second. "Well, that part was wonderful, obviously. But I realized I was meant for greater things than being trapped in a cage forever."

"You escaped?" said Joey.

"I escaped," said Brutilda. "One night, I pushed open my cage door, hid myself in the garbage can, and ran away when the janitor took it out in the morning." She paused. "There was one little girl who used to push gummy bears into my cage. I do feel bad about abandoning her." Brutilda looked down at Princess Yislene, sleeping next to her. "But I was destined for more important tasks."

"So you just decided to become a rat."

Brutilda turned a withering glare on Joey. "Life must seem so simple . . . when you're so simple."

Parsifur interjected, "Fair 'Tilda didn't 'just decide' anything. She wandered homeless for quite some time. Nearly starved to death. She only weighed about a million pounds as I recall. . . ." Brutilda scowled, but Parsifur continued. "And when I first saw her, she was about to be slaughtered by a pack of marauding Under-Realmers."

"You were there?" asked Joey.

"Aye," said Parsifur. "There was a rabid raccoon threatening our southern trade route with Peacemeal. I was part of a hunting party Uther led to end the threat. We were on our way home, exhausted from the quest, when we chanced upon the Lady Brutilda, cornered by Under-Realmers in an alley, and verging on death."

"Some of you wanted to let them kill me," said Brutilda.

"Correction, O furry sphere—*all* of us did," said Parsifur. "Except Uther, of course. We were wounded ourselves, in no shape for combat. If the Under-Realmers wanted to slay some monster they'd found"—here Brutilda stiffened—"what business was it of ours? *Hee-hee-hee.*"

"But noble Uther never saw a battle that wasn't worth fighting. Or a maiden that wasn't worth saving. And he was right, of course. He always was. Ravalon's never had a doughtier defender than our Brutilda."

"He saved me," said Brutilda, with her eyes back on the princess. "He saved me when the whole world had turned its back."

There was a long silence.

"Your conversation sparkles as always, my silky cow," said Parsifur before turning to Joey. "We should sleep while we can."

"You sleep. I'll stand watch," said Brutilda.

"Of course you will," said Parsifur, "I wasn't talking to *you.* Hee-hee-hee."

Joey did feel tired. He curled up on the ground, but guilt soon began to gnaw at him. "Are you sure it's okay to rest?"

"Relax, little savior," said Parsifur. "Brutilda will wake us up if we get an unexpected visitor."

"Maybe . . ." said a very deep voice. "Or maybe the unexpected visitor will wake you up himself."

Joey jumped to his paws and looked to see who was talking. Somehow a rat had snuck up on them. And that seemed impossible because this rat was *enormous*—nearly the size of Brutilda, but all rat. His fur was pitch-black and stuck out in sharp, jagged spikes that made him look even bigger. Long white fangs curved down from his upper jaw. Joey had seen fangs like that before. In drawings of saber-toothed tigers.

The colossal rat squatted in the entrance to the duct they were hiding in, nearly blocking the whole thing. Joey realized with a shiver that this meant the big rat was squatting in the *exit* to the duct, too. Their only way out was *through this rat.*

18

THE BIG BLACK RAT looked as solid as a wall. More solid. Walls didn't have fangs or claws.

"Now *how*," asked Parsifur, acting very cool indeed, "did you get past the cats?"

"I have a way with cats," said the giant rat.

Brutilda moved carefully forward, putting her body between the visitor and the princess. "If you're looking for a place to sleep, keep moving. This den is occupied."

The giant shook his massive head. "I'm not looking for a place to sleep. I'm looking for you."

"I see," said Brutilda, as she pulled her massive, long sword from her back.

Parsifur stepped forward so that he stood side by side with Brutilda. "We're not in the mood for guests at the moment. It might be safest for all parties," he said, drawing his paper-clip sword from his side, "especially *you*, for you to move on."

The giant didn't even blink. Compared to his bulk, Parsifur's sword might as well have been a hair plucked from an anemic flea. "Don't pick a fight you can't win," he said. He didn't say it meanly. It was just a statement of fact.

Parsifur's merry eyes darted to the sleeping princess. "Oh, this is a fight I *have* to win. And don't worry, I *will*. I always do. *Hee-hee-hee.*"

The giant rat looked at Parsifur for a second, then leaned backward a little and started *shaking*. A low rumbling noise bounced off the aluminum walls of the duct like rolling thunder. It took Joey a second to figure out what it was: *laughter*. The giant rat was *laughing back* at Sir Parsifur, and his big laugh was completely drowning out Parsifur's brave squeak. The little white rat's smile suddenly seemed a little forced.

Joey looked again at Princess Yislene, who still lay sleeping, completely defenseless. He thought of the Squagician he had to find in order to get changed back. And he thought of Mom, waiting for him to get home. He knew what he had to do, though he could barely believe he was going to do it. He pulled out Ratscalibur—it felt cool in his clammy hand—and stepped forward to join Parsifur and Brutilda. "We don't want any trouble," said Joey. "But we're not afraid to fight, either. If this is your home, I'm sorry. We'll be gone tomorrow. But for now, we're staying here," he said, holding Ratscalibur high, "whether you like it or not."

The giant stopped laughing and took a step forward. Then another. He was like a tank with arms and legs. Joey could see the rat's muscles rippling under his coarse fur. He seemed completely unafraid of Joey and Brutilda and Parsifur. He opened his coal-black eyes wide, stuck his head forward, and stared Joey straight in the face.

"Now, honcho," said the big rat. "Is that any way to greet your favorite uncle?"

IT TOOK JOEY a second to figure out what was happening. It took him another second to believe it was true. "Uncle Patrick?" he said at last.

The giant rat laughed again and held out his arms for a hug.

Joey rushed forward, and he suddenly found himself wrapped up in the Patrick-Rat's strong arms. The fur that had looked so spiky and scary was warm and soft. It even kind of *smelled* like Uncle Patrick, too: like stale beer and sweat. Which smelled just about right for a giant rat.

Joey pulled himself free and looked at Parsifur and Brutilda. They were staring at Joey like he had just chewed off his own paw. "Sir Parsifur? Brutilda? This is my Uncle Patrick."

Brutilda recovered her senses and sniffed, "Another High-Realmer? This kingdom has truly fallen on dark days." But Parsifur just giggled, like usual.

Joey was very happy to see his uncle but very confused to see him as a rat. "But . . . but *how?*"

Patrick chuckled. "Your friend Gondorff was not as dead as you probably thought."

Parsifur surged forward: "Gondorff lives? Is it true?"

Patrick stopped chuckling. "No. I'm sorry . . . no. He woke up just long enough to tell me what he had done to Joey. So I asked him to turn me into a rat, too, because . . ." Uncle Patrick scratched the fur behind Joey's ears, "Well, because I kind of like Joey and want to make sure he's safe. And so Gondorff changed me, and I'm grateful. But the effort was too much for him. He's dead now."

"But are you *sure* . . . ?"

"I checked," said Patrick. Everyone was silent for a little while.

It felt kind of cruel to be given the hope that Gondorff might be alive, just to find out he was really dead, after all.

At least Joey wasn't alone here anymore. So he started talking. He started telling Uncle Patrick *everything*. It felt good to tell someone about all the crazy things he'd been doing . . . someone who would understand just how crazy these things were. Joey talked fast, nonstop, barely taking a breath. The words just spilled out of him. Uncle Patrick didn't even try to interrupt or ask a question. But when Joey was finally done, Uncle Patrick gave him a serious look and said, "That's amazing, Joey. But I think there is probably something you want to ask me."

Joey realized that there *was* something he wanted to ask Uncle Patrick. But something he was scared to ask, too. He didn't want to know the answer. That's why he'd been talking so much, so fast . . . so he wouldn't have to ask the question. Now he was all out of words, and the question was the only thing left to say:

"How's Mom?"

MOM SAT ON the couch. She had her cell phone in her lap and the landline on the table next to her. There was no noise in the apartment except for the sound of street traffic outside. She didn't have the TV or the radio on. She didn't want there to be any noise, in case one of the telephones started to ring.

But they didn't ring. Mom wasn't crying, because she never did that. But she was breathing very slowly, in and out, in and out.

She was all alone. She didn't know anyone in the city except for Patrick. And now Patrick was missing, too.

The police had left an hour ago. They had dusted for fingerprints and examined the bars on Joey's window. But there really wasn't much they could do. They promised her they would call as soon as they found out anything. Mom could see in their eyes that they thought that Joey must be with Patrick. Maybe they had gone to a movie or something and just forgot to tell her.

Joey must be with Patrick, thought Mom. But she didn't really believe it. Why would either of them, Joey or Patrick, just disappear like that?

Mom caught a look at herself in a mirror. Her red hair was clumped like a crazy, curly nest on top of her head. It's what happened when she didn't brush her hair. She looked like a crazy person.

So Mom stood up and decided that she wouldn't be crazy anymore. She went into the bathroom and brushed her hair. Then she put on some clean clothing and did the dishes. She decided to make some coffee. That was a normal thing for her to do. Then she remembered that the coffee maker was on the floor in Joey's room.

She went to get it. She walked quickly so she wouldn't think about where she was going . . . but when she bent down to pick up the coffee pot, her eyes landed briefly on the hamster cage next to Joey's bed. The rat was still in there.

Mom walked over to the cage. The gray rat was curled up dead in the corner. She shook the cage, but the rat didn't move. She looked closely; the rat wasn't breathing. She pulled the rat out of the cage, and it was cold in her hands.
It was dead, dead, dead.

For some reason that made her sadder than almost anything, she knew she had to get the rat out of her house, immediately. So she carried it by the tail,

out the door, and down the hallway, with all the neighbors staring at her. She went to the garbage can that stood on the sidewalk outside her window, lifted the lid, and dropped the rat. Her tears fell like fat raindrops onto its dull gray fur. Then she put the lid back on, made herself stop crying, and went back into the apartment to wait by the phone.

But where was the phone? She'd left it somewhere. . . .

In a panic, she searched the living room, the kitchen, under the sofa cushions. Then she went into Joey's room. *There it was*, on the bedside table, next to the hamster cage.

It was only after she'd picked up the phone that she saw the message, scratched in tiny letters in the dust on the tabletop.

i m bringin him bak

There were paw prints leading away from it.

PARSIFUR WANTED to go back to traveling on rooftops—it was faster than walking on the sidewalk—but Brutilda said no. It was too dangerous on the rooftops. It was too easy for the Black-Claws to attack them. And keeping the princess safe was Brutilda's primary goal.

Not that walking on the sidewalk was entirely safe, either. Especially when the sidewalk was crowded with people. The cats walked single file, twisting around the legs of the pedestrians like a long, furry snake. Pants legs and bare legs and skirts towered over them. Sometimes it even seemed like some of the people saw them—usually a drunk, or a little kid (maybe they could see through the -agic?)—but nobody else ever paid any attention.

Every now and then someone would accidentally step on one

of the cats' tails, and whoever was riding that cat would have to hang on for dear life as the cat leaped like a hissing rocket. But Joey didn't mind any of it so much now that Uncle Patrick was riding right behind him. Joey hoped Squamish didn't mind carrying two rats now instead of one (especially since one of them was as big as Patrick), but the black cat never complained.

Parsifur said they'd make it to Squirrelin's lair by the afternoon if they made good time. Joey hoped they did. Not even for himself so much as for Mom. Uncle Patrick had said she was already pretty upset, but with both him *and* Patrick gone, she must have been going crazy. He was thinking about her when he felt a tap on his shoulder.

"Are you going to eat that?" asked the princess.

"Huh?" said Joey, surprised to see that she was riding alongside him.

"That," she said, pointing to a pizza crust Joey had tucked into his belt. "Are you done with it?" She'd slept all night without moving, like she was in a coma. But when she woke up she'd been full of energy and *starving*. She'd been eating ever since.

Joey had been saving the crust for later—they'd had breakfast in the pizza place's dumpster—but he knew better than to say no to a princess. "Oh, I'd forgotten it was there," he said, and handed it to her.

Yislene smiled. "You're a terrible liar, but I'm much too hungry to care. Ragic makes me absolutely famished." She smacked her mouth. "Mmm, there's a cockroach leg stuck to the cheese. Bonus!"

Joey was a little confused by Yislene. At first he'd been scared of her because she was a *princess*. And she could cast *spells*. But now, watching her wolf down cockroach parts like a kid eating tacos, he didn't know what to think. She seemed more like someone he'd be friends with at school than a princess.

Uncle Patrick seemed to be thinking the same thing as he watched her eat. "Does Ragic have that effect on all Ragicians?"

84

"Yes," said Yislene, through a mouth full of food. "But it's worse for me because I'm so young. *Ragic* is fueled by a rat's primary attribute: energy. It burns the energy right out of us, and the only way to refuel is to eat."

"And this is the way all . . . er . . . -agic works?" asked Patrick.

Yislene shook her head to say no, and swallowed her food. "Every kind of animal has a different primary attribute. So all their -agics have different fuels. For instance, the primary attribute of dogs is loyalty. So Dagic is fueled by loyalty."

That didn't make sense to Joey. "So, a . . . *Dogician* burns the loyalty out of himself when he casts a spell?"

"It's not as simple as that," said Yislene. "Dagic actually intensifies the loyalty in a Dogician. The most loyal dogs in the world are all powerful Dogicians."

"Don't you mean dalmatians?" asked Uncle Patrick.

"I don't know what that is," said Yislene.

"Just a dumb joke," said Uncle Patrick, weakly.

"Then why did you say it?" asked Yislene. But before Patrick could answer, she moved on with the conversation. "-Agic has a different effect on every species that works it. No other -agicians get as tired as we rats do, but the primary attribute of bats is hunger, so Bagicians tend to get equally hungry. . . ."

"Well, they're sort of like flying rats," said Uncle Patrick.

"*They* like to think so," sniffed Sir Parsifur, who'd snuck up on the conversation. "It seems to me they're more like featherless pigeons."

The cats climbed over a low stone wall, and the questers found themselves surrounded by tall trees covered with brown-and-orange leaves. They'd reached the park.

"Ah," said Sir Parsifur, "we've made good time. Not much longer to ride now."

Arriving at the park reminded Joey of where they were going and made him wonder something. "What's the primary attribute of squirrels?"

"Greed," said Parsifur. "All squirrels are greedy. Nothing but nuts on the brain. But Squagic makes them almost unbearable. Powerful Squagicians ... fie! Holing up in their hollow trees, surrounded by decades' worth of acorns. More than they could eat in a hundred lifetimes. And always greedy for more. Lunatics, the whole lot of 'em."

"And yet," said Uncle Patrick, "we are at this moment on a quest to see the most powerful Squagician of them all."

"You'll note," said Parsifur with a wink, "that *he's* not coming to *us* to volunteer his services."

Brutilda's low voice rolled back from the front of the line. "He'll help us ... when he hears what Salaman's done to Gondorff."

Patrick whispered to Joey, "I didn't know she was listening."

"I have ears," said Brutilda.

Joey decided to change the subject. "Do all animals do -agic?"

"Most ones with brains do," said Yislene. "Not birds or lizards, that I know of. Too dumb."

"What about cats?" said Patrick.

"Too smart," said Parsifur. Chequers purred.

Joey was annoyed. "Can't you ever give a straight answer?"

Parsifur winked. "As soon as you start asking straight questions."

The princess took pity on Joey. "There isn't much of a straight answer to give. Most intelligent animals have an -agic, some don't—"

"Possums," interjected Brutilda, giving an example.

"Just as most intelligent animals speak," Yislene continued, "and some don't. Some animals talk, some don't."

Uncle Patrick looked thoughtful. "What about people?" he asked. "Why don't we see people doing real Magic all the time?"

"You do," said the princess. "You probably see it every day. You just don't recognize it as such—and neither do they."

"Humans have never mastered their -agic properly," agreed Parsifur.

"When do we do Magic?"

"Gondorff explained this to me once," said Yislene. "He'd made a study of primitive -agics. Humans do Magic, say . . . when you think you are about to drown, but you somehow get the strength to swim to the surface. Or you bump into a friend just when you need a friend the most. Or you've lost something that you desperately need, and then you find it . . . in a place where you've already looked a thousand times."

"I've done that," admitted Uncle Patrick.

"Yes," said Yislene, "I suspect it's strong in your family. -Agic and heroic powers run intertwined through the blood. For Joey to be the great hero he is, his parents must surely be great Magicians or heroes, or both."

Joey felt less like a hero than ever before. *You were a hero because your parents were Magicians or heroes?* Well, he hadn't seen much Magic growing up, that's for sure.

Mom was definitely a hero, but not in the way Yislene meant. And though Mom never talked about Joey's dad, from the little hints that Uncle Patrick dropped, he sounded anything but heroic. Joey shared a look with Uncle Patrick, who shook his head; he was clearly thinking the same thing.

Patrick cleared his throat and changed the subject. "But what powers Magic? What's our primary attribute?"

"Oh," said Yislene, "Well . . . please don't be offended by this. A 'primary attribute' isn't the *only* thing that a species has, it's just something that a species has *more of* than other animals."

"So what's our primary attribute?" repeated Uncle Patrick.

Princess Yislene looked at Sir Parsifur, who shrugged. Then she turned to Uncle Patrick and said, as gently as possible, "The primary attribute of people . . . is sadness."

"Sadness. Huh," said Uncle Patrick. "Well, that's depressing."

Joey thought so, too. "So, we just have this weak little -agic, and it's powered by sadness."

"I said 'primitive,'" said Yislene, "not 'weak.' Your kind has never learned to *control* your Magic . . . but it can be an overwhelming force when let loose."

Parsifur grinned. "People are full of a powerful lot of sadness."

Joey frowned and opened his mouth to respond, then suddenly shouted "*Ow!!!*" A fiery poker had just stuck him in the side. He put his hand to the source of the burn— Ratscalibur—and pulled it from his belt. He held it high and watched it glow with a fierce internal heat. "Well I don't know much about Ragic," he said, "but I think we're about to be attacked. Brutilda! There are enemies near here!"

At the front of the line, the guinea pig swiveled her head like an owl, looking at the trees in every direction. "Where?" she replied. "I see noth—"

That's when the spear knocked her out of her saddle.

MORE SPEARS CAME, and quickly, whistling high out of the trees at them: *thwik thwik thwik.* Before Joey had time to think, Uncle Patrick had grabbed him and thrown them both off Squamish's back. Joey found himself deep in a pile of leaves: protected, maybe just for a second, from the flying spears.

"You okay?" asked Uncle Patrick, who was on top of him.

"Uh-huh," croaked Joey. His fangs chattered against each other. *What was happening?*

"Good," said Uncle Patrick. "Stay here." And with a roar like an animal—which Joey suddenly realized his uncle *was*—the giant black rat ran out to fight whoever was attacking them.

Uncle Patrick wasn't the only one roaring. Joey worked up the

nerve to peek out from under the leaves and saw dozens of rats pouring out of the bushes, shrieking and yelling as they came. These were lean rats, with cold eyes and rough fur. They didn't carry weapons, but some of them were wearing leather helmets, and some of them—Joey blinked—*some* of them were wearing helmets with horns sticking out of them. . . .

"Viking rats?" said Joey. *No, not Viking rats*—his stomach went cold when he realized what they really were—*sewer rats.* And so many of them . . .

Uncle Patrick was with the cats, throwing his huge body at the invaders, slashing at them with his cruel teeth. He didn't have a sword, but Joey didn't think he would use one if he did. It looked like Patrick was enjoying wrestling with the crazed rats on their own terms.

Parsifur was fighting much more daintily, dancing around on his back paws and using his sword, expertly and delicately, to trip

the attackers and spear them with its tip, until they ran off screaming and bleeding into the woods. Every attacker who fled heard
Parsifur's *hee-hee-hee* jingling in the air behind them.

Brutilda stood in one place, solid as a mountain, swinging her
enormous broadsword back and forth so that it knocked down the
Viking rats like bowling pins. She had a couple of the wild rats'
tiny spears sticking out of her chest and shoulders, but she didn't
pay any attention to them.

They all fought with their backs to each other, in a circle around
Princess Yislene, who was waving her paws in front of her mouth
and whispering again. What was she . . . oh. Joey saw that though
spears were still flying down out of the trees at his friends— *thwick
thwick*—they were now bouncing off an invisible umbrella before
they could hit anyone. The princess was throwing up a force field.

It was so terrifying (and thrilling) to watch that Joey felt like
he was right in the middle of it. So he was kind of surprised when

he realized that he *wasn't* in the middle of it *at all*. He was off to the side, stuffed under some leaves, completely forgotten. In fact, if he wanted to, he could probably just tunnel away, under the leaves, and be long gone before anyone noticed he was missing.

He had acted brave before, when he'd thought Patrick was Salaman, and he'd stood with Parsifur and Brutilda to defend the princess. But this was different. This wasn't *acting* brave. This was *being* brave. Real battle.

It didn't look like his friends really needed him, anyway. They were fighting really well. . . .

Except that no matter how many invading rats they fought off, more kept coming. A new kind of rat was attacking, too, and these ones looked crazy: long and scabby and wild-eyed, with their fur painted blue and red and other bright colors. They seemed to scream and cry and laugh, all at the same time, as they tumbled through their brown-furred brothers into battle, fighting like maniacs. They were attacking the cats mostly, crawling all over them, biting and scratching, overwhelming them. . . .

The princess's chanting was getting slower: she was getting tired. All of Joey's friends seemed to be moving more slowly, actually. Brutilda had a broad slash on her pink nose that was dripping blood. Uncle Patrick had a few of the little spears in his shoulders now, too. And Parsifur was giggling less and less.

And still the invading rats kept coming . . . and coming . . .

In front of Joey, a battle raged. Behind him, the leaves were quiet and cool . . . untouched. He could feel them almost *inviting* him to tunnel away through them, to where it was safe. He could find a hole in the stone wall around the park, cover the entrance with a rock, and be done with this battle . . . with *everything* . . . forever.

But right in front of his eyes, he could *see* his friends struggling against impossible odds. He could *hear* their breathing turn to gasps as they got tired.

And he could *feel* Ratscalibur burning in his grip.

Suddenly Joey knew that running wasn't even an option.

He leaped out of the leaves with a piercing scream and followed his sword into a wall of doom.

JOEY HAD GOTTEN beat up one time at his old school, but he hadn't even fought back, so you couldn't call that a *fight*. Now he was in more than a fight. Now he was going to war.

He had no idea what he was supposed to do.

Luckily, it seemed like his sword did.

Glowing red, Ratscalibur led him right into the middle of the Viking rats. One moment, Joey was safe in the leaves; the next he was surrounded by a sea of snarling, slobbering savages. They didn't pay any attention to Joey at first—maybe he was too small to notice—but as soon as he made his first jabs at them with his spork, they turned on him with a vengeance. A huge rat with a hole where his nose should have been lunged at Joey, swinging his claws like talons. . . .

This is the end, thought Joey.

But he also thought, *If I put my sword there I can block him.* . . .

And as soon as Joey *thought* it, Ratscalibur was *there*. The hollow-nosed rat squealed as his claws banged against the red-hot sword. He swung his other paw at Joey . . . but Ratscalibur was *there*, too. The rat shrieked with displeasure and ran away.

Others took his place. More and more and more. Big rats, small rats. Rats with empty eye sockets, rats that smelled like week-old fish. And Joey was fighting them all. Thrusting with Ratscalibur, slicing with Ratscalibur, spinning around with Ratscalibur to hack at the rats who were leaping at his back.

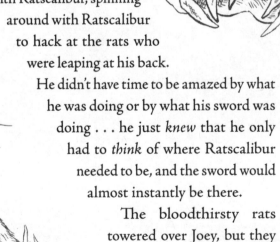

He didn't have time to be amazed by what he was doing or by what his sword was doing . . . he just *knew* that he only had to *think* of where Ratscalibur needed to be, and the sword would almost instantly be there.

The bloodthirsty rats towered over Joey, but they couldn't stop him. He slashed and slashed and slashed till they ran.

Then, through a gap in the enemy's ranks, he saw a familiar black-and-white form, curled up into a ball, howling in pain as it was overrun by red-painted wild rats. *Chequers.*

Without a thought Joey sprinted through the Vikings to the fallen cat. He leaped on her back and hacked at the biting, frothing Under-Realmers that were swarming her, cutting them, knocking them off, kicking them. . . .

Now a wild rat had its arm around Joey's neck, its head pressed next to his, with breath that smelled like something scraped from the bottom of a porta-potty—which, even to Joey's new nose, didn't smell good. The wild rat hissed, "You will die now, young one. . . ."

But before it could follow through on its threat, Ratscalibur had hacked at its fingers, slicing three of them clean off. The evil rat screamed in pain and leaped off Chequers's back to scamper into the underbrush.

Now the ground was moving under Joey's feet. *It's an earthquake,* he thought for a second, until he realized that Chequers was just getting out of her protective crouch and standing up. The cat looked back at Joey—her face was covered with rat bites and broken whiskers—and she *purred* gratefully as she shook her head, throwing the last wild rat off her ear. Then she looked forward, and Joey knew what he had to do. He sat in her saddle, grabbed the reins, and held on for dear life as she leaped into the fray.

It was all sort of a blur after that. Later, Joey remembered riding Chequers around and around the circle his friends had made around Yislene, leaning down out of his saddle to spear the invading rats. At some point Joey must have fallen off Chequers—*or was it possible he'd leaped down?*—because at the end he was on the ground, swinging his mighty sword at a blue-painted giant who would not give up until Joey sliced a hunk out of his generous belly. Then the

wild blue rat ran for the bushes. Joey looked around to see whom he had to fight next. . . .

Except there was no one left. The invaders were all gone. Nothing but their stink and their blood remained.

His friends and their cats were all scattered on the ground, wounded to various degrees, breathing heavily, too tired to talk. Yislene was lying motionless, like a statue. *Was she . . . ?* Joey knelt down next to her and smiled: she was breathing. She was just asleep.

He felt a paw on his shoulder. He looked up to see Parsifur, staring at him with serious eyes. "That," said the little white rat solemnly, "*that* . . . was some very fine swordsmanship."

Then he looked to the trees above them. "Now let's get to cover before they find more spears."

"*OW!*"

Brutilda was trying to pull a spear out of Uncle Patrick's side, and Uncle Patrick wasn't happy about it. Brutilda didn't care. "Stop whining, you big baby, and hold still."

"I will not," said Patrick. "That one's . . . stuck in something. It's not like the others." He looked down at the two bloody-tipped spears that had already been removed. They were just long slivers of sewer-soaked driftwood, crudely sharpened to points. "Just break off the end and leave the rest of it for now."

"Don't be stupid—"

"Leave it, I said. I like the way it looks."

Brutilda grunted, but she was clearly too tired to argue about it anymore. Besides the cut on her nose, there were several holes in her own hide, and she set herself to curling up and licking her wounds clean.

They were all wounded, except for Yislene, who, untouched but exhausted, was lying passed out in the middle of the cave. It wasn't a cave really—more like a hollow place beneath an old dead tree, but it was big enough for all of them, including the cats, to rest in.

Joey licked the stump of his tail. He'd been surprised to discover, once they'd gotten to safety, that someone had bitten most of it off in the battle. Joey felt bad about that; he'd kind of liked having a tail.

"I am most grateful," said Sir Parsifur, as he cleaned the gouges in Chequers's fur, "for your service to my beloved Checky in her time of need."

"It was nothing," said Joey. "Anyone would've—"

"No, they wouldn't have," said Brutilda.

"Where did you learn to work a sword like that, honcho?" asked Uncle Patrick. "Did they have a fencing team at your school or something?"

Joey shook his head. How could he make them understand? He was proud that he'd done well, but he wasn't suddenly some great *hero*. "I didn't really do anything. It was Ratscalibur that did all the work."

"Oh, sure . . ." said Uncle Patrick, like he didn't believe his nephew.

"It's true!" said Joey. "In fact, I . . ." He swallowed. This was going to be hard to say. "I . . . I almost ran away," he confessed. "I was *so* close . . . but then, you know, I just decided to stay. Ratscalibur did everything after that."

Brutilda paused from licking her fur and looked at him. Joey was scared she was going to say something terrible, about him being a coward . . . *something he deserved.* Instead she said, "The great battle was the one you fought against yourself and won. When you decided to stay. That was when you proved yourself a hero. What Ratscalibur did after that . . ." She waved her paw. "That was merely . . ."

"Icing on the cake," said Uncle Patrick.

Brutilda glared at him. "I was going to say 'a scab on the frog's guts,' but I think it means the same thing." She went back to licking her wounds.

"I think she likes you," Parsifur whispered to Uncle Patrick.

"I have ears," said Brutilda.

Joey felt something wet at his ankles. He looked down and saw Chequers's tongue, slithering around him like a pink boa constrictor. He kicked the tongue away, but gently, and smiled at her. He turned to Parsifur. "What do we do now? Wait until the princess wakes up?"

Parsifur sat down and sighed. "We can't wait that long. We're not safe in this park. I regret to say that the situation is worse than we'd thought.'"

"Why?"

"Because of the Under-Realmers," moaned Brutilda.

"So those *were* sewer rats," said Joey.

"That they were," said Parsifur. "Woe betide us."

"Who were the painted ones?" asked Uncle Patrick.

"Berzerkers. The worst of the worst. All Under-Realmers are savage, but Berzerkers lack any soul at all. They'll gnaw your face off if given half a chance." Parsifur looked with pity at his wounded cat. Chequers snuggled against him.

"Why is it so bad that sewer rats are in the park?" asked Joey.

"Because Squirrelin wouldn't allow it," boomed Brutilda. "Or he never used to. He doesn't even allow other *squirrels* in this park. Under-Realmers *here*? *Never*. And yet"—she stretched the little word out like a long low note in a song—"here they are. It . . . seems *possible* that Squirrelin's grown too old or too weak to ward them off anymore."

"Mayhap he's grown too *dead*," said Sir Parsifur.

"That is possible, also."

"And if any of these *possibilities* are true," said Parsifur, "then I'm afraid old Squirrelin wouldn't be much help to us."

"Which means," said Uncle Patrick, "that we've come all this way for nothing."

"So . . . where are we going to go for help?" asked Joey.

Parsifur exposed his daggerlike teeth. It took Joey a second to realize he was smiling. "To Squirrelin, of course."

"But you just said—"

"*Hee-hee-hee*," the white rat giggled, "You act like we have a choice!"

IT WAS LATE afternoon when they got to Squirrelin's oak. The progress was slow. The rats walked alongside their tired cats instead of riding them, except for the sleeping Princess Yislene, who was strapped onto Questel's back. Everyone seemed to be limping, or dragging. But no one complained.

Joey kept an eye out for sewer rats, even though he knew that if they decided to attack again . . . well, there wasn't much Joey or his friends could do. He tried to *sniff* for them, to get a location, but it was like his nose ran up against a wall. Hopefully they had gone back underground.

Just when Joey didn't think he could walk another step, they reached a clearing. In the center stood an oak tree. It was ancient

and enormous, tall and black, with long, twisted branches that reached out from its trunk like greedy fingers. "See there?" said Parsifur, pointing to a hole about halfway up the tree. "That's the entrance to Squirrelin's lair."

"How will we get up there?" asked Joey.

Parsifur winked. "You'll see."

Brutilda climbed up on Questel, untied the princess, and then jumped down, carrying Yislene on her back. The princess was sleeping so deeply that she didn't even stop snoring. Parsifur approached a fat brown squirrel that sat gnawing on a walnut at the foot of the tree. "Greetings, Squire Jellybelly," said Parsifur. The squirrel didn't look up or anything, just sank his teeth into the walnut and spat when the insides turned out to be rotten. Parsifur didn't look insulted. "Mind our mounts, O greedyguts, while we confer with your master. They need food, water, and cow's milk if you have it." The squirrel didn't even nod. He just stood unhappily, grabbed the reins of the cats, and led them around the back of the tree. *He must be Squirrelin's stable boy*, thought Joey.

Then Parsifur looked up, to the hole in the tree—so far above their heads that Joey could barely see it—and whistled, long, high, and piercing. There was no response. He whistled again. Finally, a

voice as dry and crackly as a falling leaf came down to them:
"No visitors."

"My liege," said Sir Parsifur, "we are a questing party come
from King Uther, and we seek to consult with your master,
Squirrelin—"

"No visitors."

"It is a matter of great importance—"

"No visi—"

"We brought presents," yelled Uncle Patrick,
interrupting the voice.

There were several seconds of complete silence. Then,
suddenly, a long rope uncoiled from the hole and came
right down to them. Brutilda grunted appreciatively and
started to climb the rope, with the princess still strapped
to her back. Parsifur gave Patrick an odd look.

Patrick said, "You don't live in this city very long without learning how to bribe a doorman." Then he said to Joey,
"Want me to carry you?"

"No," said Joey, "I can make it." As scary as climbing a
rope that high would be, Joey figured it would probably be
even scarier to do so while being carried by someone else.

The rope was longer than Joey had thought. Probably
about thirty or forty feet . . . which seemed more like three
hundred feet to someone the size of a rat. But the climbing
was easy, and Joey's little paws gripped the rope like it was
made of chewed bubble gum. Being a rat had its advantages.

Waiting at the top of the hole was a very old gray squirrel,
very skinny, with bare patches in his fur. "Is this Squirrelin?"
asked Uncle Patrick. Sir Parsifur shook his head and giggled
and pointed toward a narrow tunnel that led to the

tree's interior. They started to walk down the tunnel, but the old squirrel cleared his throat. "Oh, right," said Uncle Patrick, who dug into his fur and pulled out the last pepperoni rind he had left from the pizza parlor. "Sorry, it's all I've got." The doorman scowled, but he took the pepperoni.

The tunnel was low and dark. Joey could smell acorns at the end of it . . . and something else. Something spicy, but also dirty, and earthy, like a pepper that had been buried in mud.

He came out of the tunnel and found himself in a circular room, with a ceiling so high that he couldn't even see the top of it. *Is the whole tree hollow?* Stacked against the round walls— again, higher than his eyes could see—were acorns. Acorns upon acorns upon acorns. "There must be millions. . . ." said Joey.

"Enough to start a forest," said Uncle Patrick.

Joey's stomach rumbled. He remembered how good the acorn back at the village had tasted. *That seems like a year ago*, he thought.

The room was lit by a pale green, -agical flame that floated in the middle of the air. As Joey's eyes adjusted to the light, he could see that there were a few other things besides acorns here. Mostly junk, littering the floor on the far side of the room: a ball of kite string, a pile of dirty rubber bands, some Styrofoam peanuts, and a pink wax doll shaped like a squirrel. The doll was little, about Joey's size, and it looked even smaller because it was shaped like a *starving* squirrel. Joey could count the ribs carved into its sides. The toy maker hadn't even bothered to put any fur on it. It was altogether the strangest little toy Joey had ever seen.

Which was why it was especially strange when he saw it *breathe*.

"Squirrelin, old fellow," said Parsifur, walking up to the pink thing, "you look wonderful."

"NO VISITORS," wheezed Squirrelin—for that is who the pink thing was. Joey couldn't have been more surprised if he'd seen a rock start talking, or a cow jump over the moon.

"We're not exactly visitors, Your Pinkness," continued Parsifur, undeterred. "Call us 'emissaries' from the court of King Uther. I'm Sir Parsifur—you might remember I helped you fight off that possum invasion several summers ago. . . ."

Squirrelin breathed out with a hiss, as if to acknowledge that he remembered.

"Over there is stately, plump Brutilda. . . . Those odd fellows next to her are Joey and Patrick—they can be explained later. . . . and Sleeping Beauty, on Brutilda's back, is none other than Princess Yislene, heir to the throne of Ravalon."

The ancient squirrel cocked an eye at Yislene without bothering to move his body. "This much I already know," he said. When he spoke, it sounded like the smallest whisper possible, but it somehow filled the whole room.

"Oh," said Parsifur. "Well, we come with news. I regret to inform you that your old friend and apprentice, Gondorff the Gray—"

"Is dead," hissed Squirrelin. "You think to inform *me*? I assure you, Sir Wisecrack, there is precious little occurring outside this tree that Squirrelin the *Squagician* doesn't already know about."

"Then you know you have Under-Realmers roaming your park."

"Of course I do," growled Squirrelin. "They are here by my invitation. My plans for the wild ones are no concern of yours."

"So you know they attacked us," said Parsifur.

"That's what wild ones do," said the squirrel. "I know you survived."

"And you know why we're here," said Brutilda.

Squirrelin nodded, almost imperceptibly. "A realm is under siege." He turned an eye toward Joey. "And a High-Realmer boy wishes to regain his true form."

Joey swallowed. "You can . . . you can change me back?" He was almost scared to hear the answer.

Again, the squirrel nodded. "Come closer, boy."

Joey shuffled close to the aged squirrel. From a foot away Squirrelin was terrifying, but from an inch away he was almost unbearable. This close up, the squirrel was undeniably alive. Little black pinpricks dotted his entire body, where his fur used to be. His skin wasn't pink, it was *clear* . . . and paper thin. Joey could see tiny purple blood vessels branching out and pulsing just under the skin. And a tiny heart, just a little farther under the surface, *beating* . . . "Show it to me," hissed the squirrel.

Joey was confused. Show *what* to him?

"Hurry, hurry," said the squirrel scornfully. When Joey still didn't move, Squirrelin made an exasperated sound and said, "*Ratscalibur*, dunceling."

So Joey pulled out Ratscalibur and held it up to the ancient wizard's beady eyes. Squirrelin sniffed the sword like he was smelling a flower, and smiled. "So, it's true. Fascinating. I haven't seen this weapon since young Axel visited me during the War of the Seven Fleas. The handle wasn't broken then, of course." Before Joey could move away, Squirrelin stuck his soft pink nose into Joey's fur and inhaled deeply . . . so deeply that his cheeks blew up a little bit, like a man blowing a trumpet.

Joey was a little freaked out, but when Squirrelin let his breath out, he seemed satisfied. "Yes, there is heroism here. Fascinating, fascinating . . ." He cast an eye on Uncle Patrick, who stood protectively behind Joey. "In that one, too. But of a much more common sort . . ."

"So, it's true," said Brutilda. "He's the hero we've been waiting for. The prophecy . . . it's a true prophecy, and not just a nursery rhyme."

Squirrelin looked at Brutilda like she was an idiot. "Anything you say often enough becomes a true prophecy. That's how prophecy works."

Joey was stunned. He really *was* a hero? Then why was *chang-*

ing back and going home the only thing he wanted to do? No, not yet—he had to know that his friends would be safe. Too many questions were whirling around in his mind. "So," he asked the squirrel, "you know all about Gondorff . . . and the BlackClaws . . . and Salaman, right?"

Squirrelin smiled and nodded. Joey continued, "Then, please, tell us what we should do?"

Squirrelin stared at Joey with flat black eyes. "Give me time, young one. I must think."

"Please," said Joey, "I don't mean to rush you, but Salaman gave the kingdom a deadline of midnight *tonight*. After that, he'll send in the BlackClaws." Brutilda grunted. "And I . . . I need this to be over so I can turn back into *myself*. So I can *go home*." He heard a note of desperation in his voice. "My mom . . . my mom is all alone."

"If I say you must wait, you must wait."

"But . . ."

Squirrelin's eyes somehow turned blacker, like they could suck all the light from the room—and out of Joey. Parsifur stepped forward, between Joey and the Squagician. "Of course, if you think waiting is best, it's best."

Brutilda cleared her throat. "While you consider our options, might I ask that you use some tiny part of your power to heal us, O Squagician? We are sorely in need."

Squirrelin didn't move. But he made a noise in the back of his throat that didn't sound like "Yes."

"We hate to trouble you, wizened one," said Parsifur. "But we're in awfully poor condition. Just a little healing spell is all we ask." Squirrelin swiveled his eyes at Parsifur again, but this time the knight didn't give up. "Perhaps . . ." he said, "perhaps you could do it in memory of your beloved friend Gondorff."

Squirrelin made the noise in the back of his throat again—but this time he wasn't saying no. "Ah, poor Gondorff. It's the least I can do, I suppose. . . ." He closed his eyes and took a deep breath until his cheeks inflated again. But this time, he didn't stop there. He *kept* inhaling, long after anyone else would have stopped. After his cheeks blew up, the air spread to the top of his head, then his neck, then . . . his entire waxy skin inflated like a pink puffer fish, or a paper balloon. He was now as round as an ostrich egg—but Joey could see his squirrel-shaped skeleton floating inside. It was like looking at an X-ray. Just when Joey thought the old squirrel would *pop!* like a chewing-gum bubble, Squirrelin let out all his breath with a sudden hiss. And that's when Joey realized that he didn't hurt anymore.

Joey looked around. All his friends were standing straighter. Their cuts and scars and scrapes were gone. Yislene was yawning and opening her eyes. "Squagic," said Uncle Patrick, staring at the spearhead that had fallen from his suddenly healed side, "is powerful stuff."

Not quite powerful enough, thought Joey. He'd just noticed that his tail hadn't grown back.

"Our cats could use some healing, too," said Parsifur. "They're in your stables, in worse shape than we were."

"For Gondorff," said Joey quickly, before the squirrel could say no.

Squirrelin gave Joey a sharp look, but he blew himself up again, and when he let his breath out, Joey knew that Chequers and the other cats were feeling as good as he did.

"Now leave me," said the wizard. "I really must think. Nutkin will show you to a place where you can rest." The old doorman stepped out of the shadows and gestured toward another tunnel.

"May we have something to eat?" said Patrick. "We're half-starved—"

"Eat?" said Squirrelin. It sounded like a rattlesnake rattling. "*Eat?*"

"Bad idea," Parsifur whispered.

"*I have no food to share.*" The pink thing's heart was suddenly beating a mile a minute through its skin.

"But—" said Patrick, gesturing to the acorns that lined the walls.

"*That is my winter store. Would you ask me to starve when the Northwind blows, and the snow falls on the park like white death?*"

Uncle Patrick looked like he wanted to say something else, but Parsifur whispered, "That really isn't a question you want to answer." So Uncle Patrick just smiled and bowed to Squirrelin (who was turning an alarming shade of purple), then turned to the old doorman and cried out, "Nutkin, lead the way!"

"ASKING A SQUIRREL to share food," said Parsifur, "is not a technique likely to end in much success."

"I know that now," said Uncle Patrick.

"Asking a *Squagician* to share food," continued the white rat, as if Patrick hadn't said anything, "*that* is a technique likely to end with your brains leaking out of your ears whilst you levitate above an active volcano."

"Yeah, I get it—"

"Asking *Squirrelin* to share food—"

"*Will you shut up?*"

So Parsifur shut up . . . but he kept right on giggling: *hee-hee-hee.*

The room they were waiting in was small and dark. The floor

was covered with rubber bands and Styrofoam peanuts. "What's with all the junk on the floor?" Joey said.

"Squirrel furniture," Brutilda sniffed. "They don't care what they sleep on, as long as it's free."

"Squirrelin seems to be in good spirits," said Yislene, who was fully awake now.

"Really?" said Patrick. "He seemed kind of psycho to me."

"Oh, he's always like that," said Parsifur. "Trust me, I've seen him when he was *really* grumpy. No, he seems better and stronger than I'd dared hope. He may be able to help us after all. . . ."

"But *will* he help us?" asked Joey. "He seemed really reluctant to do that healing spell."

"Oh, squirrels never do anything the first time you ask," said Yislene.

"Be careful when they do," said Parsifur.

Yislene nodded. "The best news, I think, is that he's confirmed what I've known all along." She looked at Joey and smiled.

That made Joey uncomfortable. "Just because a squirrel says someone's a hero, doesn't mean he's a hero."

"Squirrelin would know," said Yislene.

Joey bristled. "Shouldn't *I* know?"

Brutilda scoffed. "Forgive me if I trust Squirrelin's judgment over yours. . . ."

"Yeah, but—"

Uncle Patrick put his arm around Joey's shoulders. "Seems strange to me, too, honcho . . . but this whole situation's more than a little strange. Besides, why shouldn't you be a hero?" He squeezed Joey tight. "You're kind of the best guy I know."

That made Joey feel a little better.

Yislene scrunched up her face and rubbed her belly. "He could've spared us *one* acorn."

"Now, Princess, you know better than that," said Brutilda.

"My mind knows better. My stomach doesn't." Yislene frowned and rubbed her belly again. Joey felt bad for her. Personally, he'd never been hungrier in his life, and *he* hadn't just woken up from a Ragic-induced nap. He couldn't imagine how hungry Yislene must feel.

"Let us hope we won't have to wait here long," said Parsifur.

Yislene put on a brave smile. "Yes, I'm sure I can last a little while longer."

Something about the way she smiled made Joey feel worse for her than ever. "I'll get you something to eat, Princess," he said, before he could stop himself.

The princess smiled, but this time for real. "Oh, Joey, are you sure?"

Joey couldn't back out now. Besides, if he was supposed to be a hero, he might as well start acting like one. "I'm sure. I can smell food hidden all over this tree." Uncle Patrick had a worried look on his face, but before he could say anything, Joey said, "I'll be fast. Squirrelin will never find out. I promise."

Uncle Patrick still looked unconvinced, and Parsifur said, "If you're caught, Squirrelin will be furious. It could jeopardize our whole mission."

"I won't get caught," said Joey. "And anyway, we can't let the princess suffer."

Uncle Patrick and Parsifur looked at each other and nodded. "No, we can't do that," said Patrick. "But be careful."

"I will," said Joey.

The princess looked worried now. "Joey, I take it back. I'm not hungry. I command you to stay here—"

"Too late," said Joey, feeling almost heroic. He sniffed the air . . . and his nose instantly told him where to go. "There's a storeroom full of all kinds of food just down the hallway a little bit. I'll be right back."

The princess smiled at him again, and Joey hurried out of the room, wondering if it was possible for him to blush through his fur.

The tunnel was empty, except for more "squirrel furniture" strewn here and there. Apparently, Squirrelin didn't have a lot of servants or family living with him. Maybe only Nutkin—and he seemed almost as old and crazy as the *Squagician* himself. There was no light in the tunnel—Squirrelin probably didn't want to waste the *Squagic*—so Joey was entirely reliant on his nose.

He passed one room that was full of something that smelled foul, even to him. Out of curiosity, he overcame his distaste and stuck his nose in the door for a better sniff. *Bird droppings.* The room was full of a mountain of bird droppings. *Disgusting.* Squirrels really would collect anything.

The next room he passed smelled a lot better, but not like food. He looked in and saw huge piles of paper clips, bottle caps, handkerchiefs, shoelaces, and other "treasures" from the park outside.

The next room was the one he was looking for. It was big, nearly as big as Squirrelin's acorn throne room, only this room didn't just hold acorns. There were half-eaten Twinkies and dog biscuits and hambones, olive pits and popcorn kernels and watermelon seeds, potato chips and licorice whips and fish heads, all mushed together into a sea of supreme deliciousness. *My goodness, Squirrelin is rich,* thought Joey. *And greedy.* It suddenly struck him how ridiculous it was that the *Squagician* wouldn't even spare one acorn. Joey felt like diving into the food and eating until he burst. But he was on a mission for the princess. His stomach would have to wait.

He saw a pizza crust about halfway up the pile and, remembering Yislene's fondness for such things, climbed up to get it (allowing himself to nibble a corn chip as he did so). He was just grabbing the crust when he saw something at the very top of another nearby peak in the pile. *Ooh, that looks yummy.* He leaped over to the other pile, scrambled up to the top, and sure enough . . . it was a jelly bean. A green jelly bean.

It seemed *right* to Joey that he should get to eat a green jelly bean here, after almost dying trying to get one back at the village. He picked up the jelly bean and stared at it like it was a huge diamond, entranced by its beauty. He was so hungry that everything about it seemed *perfect*: even the little flecks of mayonnaise on its bottom . . . the teeth marks where a human had bitten into it before spitting it out . . . the faint claw marks, scratched across its surface . . .

. . . like a rat had tried to grab it, only to be pulled away from it at the last second.

Joey wasn't hungry anymore. But he was very sure of one thing. This was the same jelly bean.

28

JOEY RAN into the room where the others were waiting, holding the jelly bean in his mouth. Yislene's face lit up with a radiant smile. "Oh, Joey—I could eat it all in one gulp!"

"Not yet," said Joey, after he'd dropped it on the floor. "It's evidence."

As quickly (and as quietly) as he could, he explained where he'd last seen this jelly bean. On a blanket as part of the Tribute, which was taken away by the BlackClaws.

Parsifur looked grim. "Are you sure, lad? Think. Are you *really* sure? Jelly beans do tend to look alike." Slowly, Joey put his paw into the grooves on the jelly bean's surface. His claws fit perfectly.

The room went silent. Joey wasn't sure for how long. It could have been just a second. It could have been hours. But he could feel the silence pressing in on him as everyone in the room realized what this meant.

Uncle Patrick was having trouble puzzling it out. "I thought you said the BlackClaws were taking the Tribute back to Salaman."

Joey nodded.

"But if the Tribute is *here*, then that means that *Squirrelin* is—"

"Ssh!" intoned Brutilda. "Don't say anything aloud that you don't have to." She looked around the room. "Who knows what the wizard hears?"

Joey turned to Parsifur and whispered. "You said Sala"—here he cut himself off—"you said he was a *Ragician*."

"We never saw him. We assumed he was, because he was so powerful." Parsifur made a sad giggle. "Did you know that rats' secondary attribute, after energy, is *arrogance*?"

Uncle Patrick looked at Joey. "I thought that sword of yours turned hot when you got around enemies. Shouldn't it have tipped you off about Squirrelin?"

Joey nodded. "I thought that at first, too. Now I think it only gets hot when I'm about to be attacked."

Parsifur had made a decision. "Princess," he said, "summon Sir Aramis."

"He'll never get here in time to save us," said Yislene.

"If anyone can find a way, it's Aramis," said Parsifur.

"Even if he did get here, what could he do?" said Patrick. "We need to get out of here *right now*."

"No," said Parsifur, "what we need to do *right now* is think. We may be trapped in the lair of the world's most powerful worker of -agic . . . whom we've just discovered is our mortal enemy—"

"*Ssh!*" ssh-ed Brutilda.

"But at least we now know what we know. And he *doesn't* know we know what we now know. So we have an advantage."

"I can't tell if you're joking or being serious," said Uncle Patrick.

"A little of both," said the white rat. *"Hee-hee-hee."* The giggle was music to Joey's ears. Maybe they still had a chance.

Yislene had been wiggling her fingers and whispering again. Now she opened her eyes. "I've sent the call to Sir Aramis."

"Did he get the message?" asked Joey.

"I have no idea!" said Yislene, looking annoyed. "Am I inside his brain?"

"Oh," said Joey. Then he asked, "Are you mad at me?"

"Yes," said Yislene.

"Why?"

"You still haven't given me that jelly bean."

He kicked it over to her, and she gleefully sank her teeth into it. She was licking her lips when Nutkin came into the room and dolefully announced, "The master will see you now."

29

EVERYTHING LOOKED the same in Squirrelin's acorn room. But everything was different. Before, Squirrelin had only *looked* scary. Now Joey knew that he had every reason to be scared of him.

"I trust you had a pleasant rest," said the ancient wizard, as they entered.

"Yes," said Parsifur, "it really helped clear our heads."

"Squirrelin," said Yislene, stepping forward, "I was too sleepy to thank you properly earlier. So let me say thank you now. For your hospitality and more. In this time of crisis, it is truly a blessing that my father and his kingdom have a friend like you."

"That is unnecessary, my dear," said Squirrelin, staring at her.

"On the contrary, it is very necessary," said Yislene, staring back. *Was she trying to fool Squirrelin into thinking she didn't know the truth? Or just make him feel guilty for betraying them?* Joey wasn't sure. Maybe Yislene wasn't sure herself.

After a few seconds, Squirrelin said, "Well. You're very welcome. And now . . . I've decided on the best way to proceed. First, I need the two High-Realmers to come closer."

Joey and Uncle Patrick exchanged a glance, then approached the ancient squirrel. "Show me your right paw, each of you." Joey and Patrick each held out their right paw. "Now," said Squirrelin, "do you give this paw willingly—"

"Wait," said Joey. That sounded familiar. "What are you doing?"

"He's changing you back," said Yislene, like it wasn't a big deal at all.

Squirrelin nodded. "You've been very helpful so far, no doubt, but this is Low Realm business. Your presence complicates matters, *Squagically*-speaking."

"Won't we be a little cramped in here?" asked Uncle Patrick, looking around the room.

Squirrelin scowled. "You'll find yourself in the park when you've transformed. Believe me, I've done this before."

"This feels wrong," said Joey. "Can't we wait a little while? You said I was a hero, right?"

Squirrelin's scowl deepened. "You've already been a hero. You've gotten your friends to me, to safety. Now your journey is over. It is time for you to return to the High Realm. I will protect your friends from now on."

No, you won't, you'll destroy them, thought Joey. *You're Salaman.* Joey could feel his friends (and Uncle Patrick) looking at him. What was he supposed to do?

"Hurry," said Squirrelin. "I won't make this offer again."

Joey and Uncle Patrick exchanged a glance. Patrick looked almost as unhappy as Joey felt, but he shrugged and said, "I came here to bring you back to your mom. This might be our only chance."

"Go ahead, young one," said Sir Parsifur. "This isn't your fight."

"But—"

"It's okay, Joey," said Yislene. "We can take care of ourselves. Get yourself to safety while you can." She smiled very bravely. Brutilda, standing beside Yislene, nodded.

Joey thought about Mom, waiting for him at home. He really *should* go back to her. Back to the apartment, and school, and signing up for Spanish class . . . he should go back to the rest of his life. . . .

Except *every day* he would think about the friends he had left here.

And what kind of life would that be?

Joey put his hand down. "Thank you, Squirrelin. But I think I'm needed here for the time being."

Uncle Patrick said, "You sure, kid?"

"I'm sure."

Uncle Patrick smiled and lowered his hand. "Then I'm sure, too." He winked at Joey. Parsifur, Yislene, and Brutilda—*even Brutilda*—were smiling, also. It even looked like Brutilda might be crying a little, but Joey knew that wasn't possible.

Squirrelin was not smiling. He was looking deeply at Joey, like he could probe his mind. And Joey had a sudden feeling that Squirrelin understood exactly *why* Joey was staying. "I see," said the Squagician. "In that case . . ."

Two things happened at once: Squirrelin started to take a very deep breath, and Ratscalibur started to burn into Joey's side like the sun.

RATSCALIBUR HAD NEVER burned like this before. Joey doubled over from the pain. Before he could even guess what was happening, Yislene started chanting—out loud this time—and waving her hands crazily in front of her face. As Squirrelin swelled bigger and bigger, her chanting got louder and louder. Joey could feel competing waves of power washing over him, but he was helpless to do anything about it.

Joey wanted to scream *What's going on?*, but his whole body was frozen. He forced his eyes to turn toward Uncle Patrick and saw him gritting his teeth as he tried to move. He was a statue, too. Smoky pink energy radiated out at them from Squirrelin . . . then was pushed back by warm yellow sunshine that seemed to

come from Yislene. The air smelled like electricity, like they were stuck inside a cloud in a thunderstorm, like lightning could strike at any second. . . .

And then it was over. Squirrelin let out his breath, but not in a big hiss like before. This time, it was like a balloon deflating because the knot came untied: *thhpppt*.

And Yislene collapsed to the floor. *Thump*.

Ratscalibur had gone instantly cool, and Joey was able to move now.

"What was that?" asked Uncle Patrick.

Joey knew. "He was trying to kill us. The princess stopped him."

The little *Squagician* was bright red with fury. "That insolent bit of fluff!" he raged. "To think that she could thwart *me*?! Well, she only had one of those in her. Let's see her stop me now!"

He started to breathe in again, and Ratscalibur resumed burning. Joey put his hand on the sword, but before he could lift it, he was unable to move again.

Joey strained with every muscle in his body, but it was no use. He was frozen. And Squirrelin was swelling bigger and bigger. . . .

This is the end.

And then a loud, commanding voice rang out through the room.

"Squirrelin, desist! This has gone far enough." The voice sounded familiar, but Joey couldn't turn his head to see who it was.

Squirrelin kept inflating, and the voice said again, "Enough!"

Squirrelin seemed to hear it that time. Now, only halfway inflated, he let out his breath with a sad sigh. Ratscalibur stopped burning. And Joey could move again. He turned his head to see who had saved him.

Sir Aramis was standing in the doorway. The vizier looked completely unafraid, like this was a situation he faced every day. "Brutilda, tend to your mistress," he commanded. The guinea pig was instantly kneeling by Yislene's side, trying to make her comfortable.

Aramis was staring sternly at Squirrelin. The *Squagician* was staring back, with barely controlled rage.

"Who is that guy?" asked Uncle Patrick.

"Sir Aramis, vizier to King Uther," said Sir Parsifur. There was not a hint of mockery in his voice. "It is a great pleasure to see you, good sir."

"Thank you," said Aramis, though he kept his eyes firmly on Squirrelin.

"Yeah," said Joey. "That was . . . um . . . *really* good timing."

Aramis shrugged and walked a little ways into the room.

"Excellent timing," said Parsifur. Then Parsifur got a funny look on his face. "In fact, it's . . . *peculiarly* good timing." Parsifur looked like he wanted to say something but hesitated. Then he went ahead, anyway. "Forgive me for asking, but . . . the princess sent her message to you a scant half hour ago. No one has more faith in your abilities than I, but . . . how did you possibly get here so quickly?"

"Oh, that," said Aramis, who finally turned to look at the white rat. "Well, you see," he nodded to someone standing outside, "I got a ride from some friends."

After a pause, a sleek black head—with a cruel black beak and dead black eyes—poked through the door.

It was a BlackClaw.

THE REST OF the bird followed the head through the door, then straightened up and stretched its wings while making an ugly *caw caw caw*. Another crow, equally big and scary, came through the door. They were linked together at the legs by a harness.

Parsifur nodded. "I feared as much."

"What's going on?" said Joey. "I don't understand. . . ."

Brutilda and Uncle Patrick looked just as confused as Joey did. Aramis had an expression on his face like he was kind of proud and kind of embarrassed. Parsifur just looked disappointed.

"It's simple, really," said Parsifur. "Salaman isn't *one* villain. He's *two*. A powerful *Squagician* and a valiant knight." The mockery had returned to Parsifur's voice. Especially on the word *valiant*.

Brutilda covered the princess protectively and looked up at Aramis, so angry she was shaking. "Betrayer . . ."

Aramis seemed a little sad. "It wasn't supposed to happen like this."

"*Hee-hee-hee*," giggled Parsifur, also a little sadly. "How *else* could it have happened?"

"Can I kill them now?" asked Squirrelin.

Aramis shook his head. "Let me try to reason with them." Aramis turned to Parsifur. "The plan was for 'Salaman' to demand a new king for our realm."

"You," said Parsifur.

"Me." Sir Aramis nodded. "Salaman was going to say that Uther is cursed, and thus the kingdom is cursed, until I take the throne. The kingdom would be so desperate by that point that they'd agree. You know how loyal the peasants are to Uther. It was the only way I could get them to turn on him."

"You can't be king," said Brutilda. "You're not of royal blood."

"No, I'm not," said Aramis, "but my queen will be." He nodded to the slumbering Yislene. "When she's old enough, of course."

Brutilda's silky hair bristled, like porcupine spikes. Joey felt the same thing happening to the fur that ran down his back.

"Surely," said Sir Aramis, "you realize that this is all for the best—"

Joey interrupted—something had just occurred to him. "When you saved Yislene from the BlackClaw . . . you just did that because you needed her alive so you could be king."

Aramis nodded again. "I felt a bit guilty about taking credit for that act of 'heroism.' I was never in any real danger. It was all play-acting and conversation when we were 'fighting.' Actually, the BlackClaw was supposed to be targeting *you*, but"—he stroked the nearest BlackClaw's wing—"well, we don't love them for their brains."

"Why me?" said Joey.

"Because of what you represent. Gondorff was meant to be the kingdom's last chance. His death was going to devastate the masses and make our whole plan possible. But *then* . . ." Aramis looked at Joey with annoyance. "But then there was a new hope."

"And you," said Parsifur, turning to Squirrelin. "What did you get out of this?"

The little wizard seemed unashamed. "Isn't it obvious? I get tribute from an entire kingdom, in exchange for one little tin crown. Indeed, Aramis is raising a force that will bring me tribute from *many* kingdoms. It was not an offer I could refuse."

"But *Gondorff*?" said Brutilda, like it was a curse. "You were willing to murder your student, your friend, to satisfy your greed?"

Squirrelin shrugged. "You can't grow a forest without burying a few walnuts." A little defensively he added, "I'm getting older. I'm not as strong as I once was. In a few hundred years, I'll want to stop working. I have to start thinking about saving up for my retirement."

Parsifur chuckled mirthlessly. "Oh, my tiny friend. It appears that the Squagic has finally won the battle for what was left of your soul."

"A soul," said Squirrelin, "is a luxury I cannot afford."

"I don't believe it," said Uncle Patrick.

"What?" said Joey.

"These guys are as bad as *people*." He shook his head. "I'm never throwing popcorn to squirrels in the park again, I can tell you that."

"No," said Parsifur, giving Patrick a funny look. "You probably aren't. *Hee-hee-hee.*"

"Let's not be too hasty," said Sir Aramis. "Why fight? Come to my side and help me reign over a new golden age. Surely you can understand my motivations. We have an ailing kingdom, suffering

131

under the rule of a sick king, whose heir is not yet old enough to rule. I did this not out of ambition. I did it for the good of the kingdom!"

Parsifur nodded. "It's a plausible yarn. And yet . . ." He looked at Joey. "Well, hero, what do you think?"

Joey shook his head. "It stinks."

"Why do you say that?"

Joey said. "Because I'm starting to learn how these guys think." He gestured to Squirrelin. "And I'm willing to bet that the only reason King Uther is sick is that someone is using Squagic on him." Squirrelin's face crumpled like he'd been slapped, and Joey knew that his guess was right.

"And," said Joey, turning to Aramis, "if Sir Aramis is really just a noble guy who's trying to save the realm, what's this *force* Squirrelin says he is collecting to conquer other kingdoms?" From the look on Aramis's face, Joey knew that he was on the right track. "I bet that *he's* the reason there are sewer rats aboveground."

Parsifur gasped in realization. "Every emperor needs an army."

Squirrelin looked at Aramis, like he was asking permission for something. Aramis sighed, then nodded and said, "Do what you must. Everyone but the girl."

Instantly, Ratscalibur burned like a branding iron in Joey's grip, and in a flash Joey knew what he had to do. Before the Squagician could even begin inflating, Joey poked him in the neck with the pointy ends of the spork. He didn't even poke him very hard. Just enough to leave four little holes in the paper-thin skin . . .

Squirrelin started gulping air like before. His cheeks swelled a little. He gulped more . . . but now, before he could inflate, the air was leaking out through the holes in his neck. *Sssss.* The tiny pink wizard grew scarlet with frustration. He kept trying to inhale faster and faster and *faster*, but still the air ran out: *sssssssssssssssssss.*

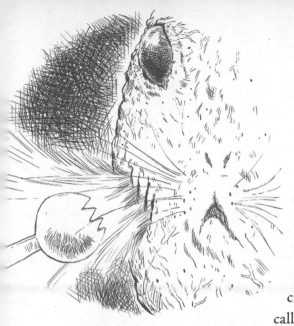

Sir Aramis ran to his partner's side. "What . . ."—he turned to Joey—"what have you *done?*"

"Marvelous," said Sir Parsifur. "But I think it's time we left." Brutilda hoisted the princess onto her back and moved toward the exit.

"Don't even think it!" screamed Aramis, as he crouched by Squirrelin, frantically trying to plug holes. "There's no escape. The park swarms with my Under-Realmers. Even now hundreds of them are climbing the rope to confront you."

"Then we will die fighting," said Brutilda, as she started to draw her broadsword. But Uncle Patrick put a hand on her arm, stopping her. "No," he said, "I think I know a way out."

"Impossible. How?"

Patrick smiled. "Let's just say I have some friends."

IN THE LIGHT OF the full moon, the rope leading up to Squirrelin's lair looked like a thick vein, pulsing poison upward. But it wasn't poison. It was rats. Long, scabby, scarred sewer rats covered the rope in waves moving up, up, up. Some of them carried little spears in their mouths, but most had no weapons except for their teeth and claws. Blue- and red-painted Berzerkers scrambled madly upward, clambering over the backs of their brethren, kicking some of them off the rope in their haste to reach the top. No one stopped for the fallen rats. No one offered any help.

A mangy gray brute was the first to reach the entrance hole, and he squeaked with triumph at having beaten the others. But

his squeak turned to a squeal of confusion
when a sleek black head with a cruel black
beak and wild, panicked eyes poked its head out,
quickly joined by another that looked even more frenzied.
From inside the hole, behind the crows, voices yelled, "Ya!
Go! Go!" With squawks of displeasure the crows leaped
from the hole and spread their wings. Hanging on to the
harness that stretched between their legs were four rats
and a guinea pig.

"Go! GO!" shouted Joey, prodding the crow on the
left with Ratscalibur.

"Ya! YA!" yelled Parsifur, prodding the crow on the
right with his sword. Brutilda was between them, expertly
knocking aside the crows' beaks with her broadsword when-
ever they craned their necks to try to peck at the pesky rats.
Uncle Patrick sat next to her, carrying Yislene on his back.

"Go! Go! Ya! YA!"

The tied-together birds lifted herky-jerkily into the air
like a drunken bat and flew crazily out of the park. When
Patrick had prodded the crows down the exit tunnel, as
Brutilda held Aramis at bay with her sword, it had been
anyone's guess if they could fly with so many passengers riding
on their harness. The answer appeared to be *yes*—but barely.

The wild rats clinging to the rope watched them go with
disappointment. One Berzerker turned sadly to another
and asked, "Well, who are we going to kill *now?*"

Up in the air, Joey thought he might end up getting
killed, anyway. There was a little seat in the middle of the
harness that must have been for Aramis to sit in when

the crows were carrying just him. It probably would have been very comfortable for Aramis: one rat carried by two big crows. But now the crows were carrying *five* rodents. Two of the rodents were enormous. And two of the rodents were stabbing the crows in the butt with swords.

This was not a comfortable ride.

"I feel like a flea in a hurricane," moaned Brutilda. The crows were trying with all their might to shake off their unruly passengers.

"C-can't hold on much longer," said Uncle Patrick, who was holding Yislene with one arm and holding on to the harness with the other. He was having the hardest time of any of them. But, of course, it had been *his* idea to borrow Sir Aramis's friends.

"Just a little bit more," said Parsifur. "Let us find a nice place to land." It was impossible to steer the crows, but they had at least flown out of the park, and now the bright lights of the city jiggled beneath them. The flight was so bouncy and disjointed it was impossible to actually *know* where in the city they were, but they just needed to see the one right thing. . . .

"Now?" asked Joey, as a rooftop suddenly appeared, only a few feet beneath them.

"Now!" shouted Parsifur.

They each swung their swords and sliced through the strings tying the harness to the crows' feet. Suddenly they were falling, but it was only a couple of feet down to the nice soft tar on an apartment building's roof. The BlackClaws, suddenly free, cawed with relief and climbed into the night sky.

"Is everyone all right?" asked Joey. Everyone nodded. No one seemed to be suffering from anything worse than a few bumps and scratches. "And Yislene," said Joey, "is she okay?"

He tilted the princess's head to see if she was breathing. Yislene made an annoyed sound, said, "Five more minutes," and started snoring again.

"So brave . . ." said Brutilda, with admiration.

"She's not brave," said Uncle Patrick. "She's in a coma." Brutilda glared at him.

Parsifur was making plans already. "Our first order of business must be to get home and warn the kingdom. I highly doubt that Aramis will give up his dreams of conquest now."

"I know where we are," said Joey, staring off the roof.

"Eh?" said Parsifur. "Where we *are* is unimportant. All we need to do is sniff, and that will tell us where we need to *go*."

"Where we are is important to me," said Joey. He turned to face the others. "And if I'm a hero, then this must be fate." He pointed to the building across the street. "That's where I live with my mother."

MOM SAT ON the couch. On the table next to her were the apartment's landline, her cell phone, and a cold cup of coffee.

Her eyes were red from crying. Streaks of gray hair had appeared in her red curls overnight. She looked like she had lost ten pounds in the two days Joey and Patrick had been gone.

Two days? Was it really only two days?

The police had come by earlier, but they were only being polite. They had no clues at all. Patrick hadn't been to his apartment or used his credit cards. No one in the city had reported seeing a big man or a little boy with a gray streak in his hair.

And she couldn't bring herself to tell them about the message in the dust. *The one that was written in Patrick's handwriting.* She must be going insane.

"We're still hopeful," the police had said, but she could tell they really weren't. It was like they were telling her, without actually saying it, *This is a big city. People go missing all the time.*

Could they really be gone? *Forever?*

Mom didn't know what she'd do. How could she go on living without her family? How could she go on without even knowing what had happened to them?

All she could do now was sit. And wait. And wait.

They had to come back. They had to come back.

JOEY AND PATRICK stood on top of the garbage can outside Mom's window, peering in. They didn't say anything for a long time.

Finally, Uncle Patrick cleared his throat and said, "She's always been so strong."

Joey knew what he meant. It just seemed impossible to believe that Mom could be so *sad*. "Do you think I made the right choice?" he asked. "When Squirrelin said he would change us?"

"I think you made the only choice you could."

Joey wished he could believe that was true.

"We must go," said Brutilda, who was standing guard over Yislene on the sidewalk next to the garbage can.

"Do try to be a bit less abrupt, O spherical one," said Sir

Parsifur, who was standing next to her. Then, apologetically, he said, "But she's right. We have to hasten back to Uther's court, and we have no cats to carry us. The princess will slow us down, as well." They'd tried to wake her up, but it was hopeless.

Patrick called down to them, "One more minute."

"One more," replied Parsifur.

Joey was still staring at Mom. "Maybe I could try to go in . . . and talk to her? Maybe she could help us?"

Patrick sighed. "She'd just think she was going crazy. You don't want to put that on her, too, do you?"

Joey shook his head.

"Look," said Uncle Patrick. "Maybe if we live through all of this, we can find another -agician—like, a Dogician, a Crocodile-ician, a nuclear fission, whatever—who can change us back."

Joey nodded.

"At the very least, we can write her a letter. Make up some excuse about where we've gone. Maybe she wouldn't feel so bad, then."

"What would we say?"

Uncle Patrick shrugged. "We'll think of something. Let's just . . . worry about staying alive first."

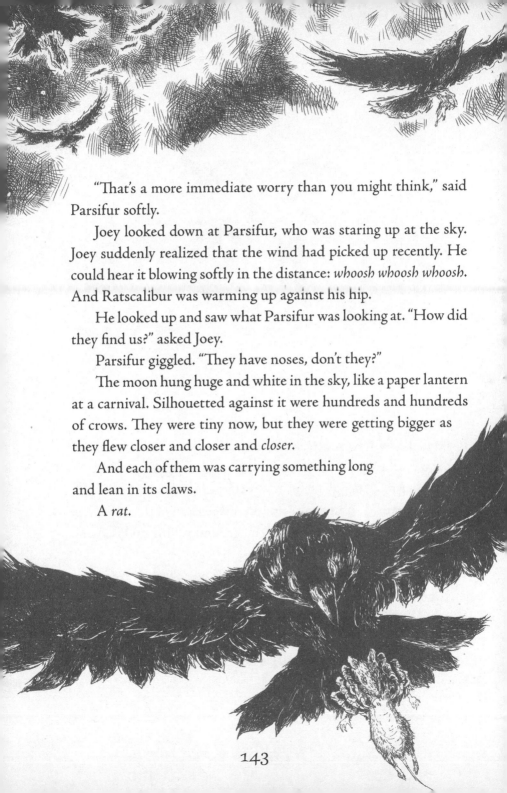

"That's a more immediate worry than you might think," said Parsifur softly.

Joey looked down at Parsifur, who was staring up at the sky. Joey suddenly realized that the wind had picked up recently. He could hear it blowing softly in the distance: *whoosh whoosh whoosh*. And Ratscalibur was warming up against his hip.

He looked up and saw what Parsifur was looking at. "How did they find us?" asked Joey.

Parsifur giggled. "They have noses, don't they?"

The moon hung huge and white in the sky, like a paper lantern at a carnival. Silhouetted against it were hundreds and hundreds of crows. They were tiny now, but they were getting bigger as they flew closer and closer and *closer*.

And each of them was carrying something long and lean in its claws.

A *rat*.

35

RIGHT BEFORE the attack, there was absolute silence. It seemed like the volume had been turned down on the entire universe.

And then, suddenly, a screaming came across the sky. The Black-Claws dropped the rats in waves, like a squadron of paratroopers. The wild Under-Realmers fell to the ground yelling and howling with rage and delight.

Joey and his friends huddled behind a makeshift fort: two garbage-can lids, leaning up against the wall. They all knew the fort wouldn't hold for long. The Under-Realmers were pounding on the lids and sticking their long snouts in the cracks between them. Joey and Parsifur were busy spearing them with their swords, keeping them back.

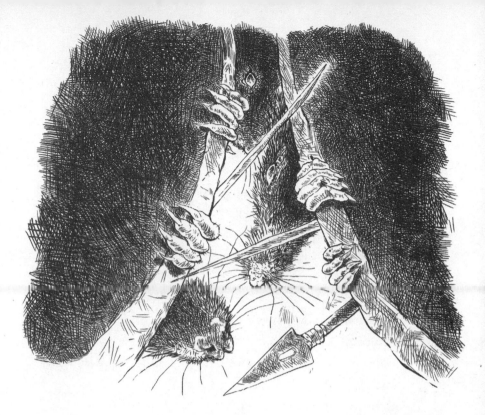

Above the din of the raging rats, they could hear one sensible voice, yelling over and over again, "*Not the girl! Do not harm the princess!*"

So Aramis was leading them himself.

"Parsifur? What should we do?" asked Joey, as he stabbed at the invaders.

"I don't know," answered the white rat. "*You're* the hero."

Joey opened his mouth to tell Parsifur to stop joking around . . . when the reality of the situation finally hit him. Here he was, fighting to the death. Against an army of bad guys. With a magic sword. To save a princess.

He really *was* the hero.

He thought that was funny. So he giggled. *Hee-hee-hee.*

The others stared at him for a second, with their mouths hanging open. Brutilda said, "That's a bad habit. Don't start."

Joey said, "I don't think I'm going to have enough time to pick up any bad habits." Then he said to Parsifur, "If this is how it ends, I don't want to die behind a wall. Let's get out there and take the fight to them."

Parsifur nodded and said, "I agree completely, my liege."

"I can't leave the princess," said Brutilda.

"I understand," said Joey.

"I'll stay with Brutilda," said Uncle Patrick.

"Five more minutes," said Yislene.

Then everybody laughed a little. Joey looked around at the group. "I'm a little too busy here to hug anyone . . . but I want you to know, I love all of you."

"We love you, too, honcho," said Uncle Patrick, like there was something in his throat.

"Well. Sir Parsifur . . . shall we?"

"After you, Sir Joey."

And with that, the two knights pushed aside the garbage lids and dashed out into the invading army.

THIS IS LIKE SWIMMING, thought Joey. *Swimming in rats.*

The two friends were completely surrounded. They fought with their backs pressed against each other so no one could attack them from behind.

They were outnumbered, hundreds to one. The only thing keeping them alive was the fact that *all* the sewer rats couldn't attack them at once. The six or eight Under-Realmers they were fighting at any given time acted as an accidental wall, getting between them and the other rats outside the circle. And the BlackClaws couldn't get through the rats.

Once again, Joey felt like he had only to *think* of where Ratscalibur needed to be, and the sword was *there*. He was cutting through the Under-Realmers like butter. But they kept coming and coming

and *coming.* . . . "Ow!" said Joey, as a Berzerker's claw tore through his right ear.

"The game wouldn't be any fun if it didn't come with a little pain," shouted Parsifur. He *had* to shout. The noise on the street was enormous. No amount of ·agic could hide the sight of hundreds of rats and crows from human eyes. The air was full of the sound of people screaming and horns honking and car alarms shrieking. The passing cars seemed to have chased off most of the crows, too, so that was in their favor. But it was pretty much the *only* thing in their favor.

So Joey fought and fought and fought, unaware that a few feet above his head, his mom was looking out the window, watching what to her seemed to be pure chaos—a sea of crows and rats, swarming mindlessly.

"Have you ever been in a fight like this before?" yelled Joey.

"Only in my nightmares," shouted Parsifur. "Or is it my dreams? *Hee-he—*"

Parsifur's giggle ended abruptly, with a gasp. Joey felt his friend slump against his back, then fall down to the ground at his feet. He looked over: a sewer rat had just taken an enormous bite out of Parsifur's side. Blood was flowing freely on the ground.

This is it, thought Joey. *The last stand.*

He stood over Sir Parsifur and turned in circles, warding the filthy rats away. "Back! Back!" he yelled. "Stay back!" The Under-Realmers were laughing now, and they were suddenly in much less of a hurry. They knew they had won. It was just a matter of time now. *It's all so unfair,* thought Joey. *They hadn't been beaten. They'd been cheated—tricked!—by their so-called friends.* . . . It made him furious. And he found himself shouting, "Where is your king?!" as he turned in his circles. The rats just laughed louder.

So Joey shouted louder. "*Where is your king?*" He waved Ratscalibur around, to emphasize his point. "*Where is the one who says he should be king, but needs an ARMY to defeat a little kid? WHERE IS YOUR KING?!*"

A quiet, calm voice cut through the noise: "Here I am."

Joey turned. Aramis was standing there, leaning on his sword. "Here I am," he repeated. "What do you want of me?"

The sewer rats suddenly hushed.

"Sir Aramis." Joey smiled. He was shaking to bits on the inside, but outwardly he smiled. "I challenge you to a duel."

Aramis threw back his head and laughed. "I admire your bravado. Certainly, I'll grant your request. It seems to me that you've earned the right to die with some honor." Aramis raised his sword.

"That's generous of you," said Joey, and he raised Ratscalibur.

Aramis leaped at him instantly, like a snake. Joey dodged the vizier and batted his sword away, just in the nick of time. Soon he and Aramis were circling each other, their swords clashing with a strangely cheerful sound: *clink clank clink.* This wasn't like fighting sewer rats. Aramis was tricky, and fast. Every stab he made felt like the first move of ten more stabs he had planned. Joey was exhausting himself, both physically *and* mentally, like he was playing soccer and chess at the same time.

It was kind of fun . . . if he didn't think about how it would end.

Clack! The tip of Aramis's sword nearly stabbed through Joey's heart, but Ratscalibur knocked it away at the last second. Aramis backed away and paused. He had a serious look on his face. "Who taught you that?" he asked.

"Taught me what?" asked Joey.

"When you blocked my thrust," said Aramis. "That was a

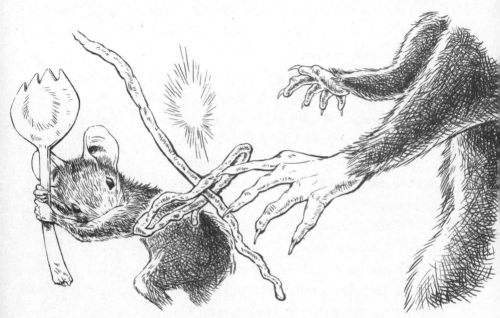

Moustoffsky Cross." Aramis could tell by Joey's face that the words didn't mean anything to him. That seemed to annoy him, and he continued, "I had to go to Prince Egbar's duchy to learn that move. And I was taught by Moustoffsky himself."

"I just . . . *did* it," said Joey.

"Less talking, more killing!" yelled a sewer rat.

"Yaaaaargh!!!" yelled a Berzerker.

"As you wish," said Sir Aramis, and he launched himself at Joey again. This attack was even more furious than before. It seemed like Aramis was determined to end this quickly. Joey found himself backing up under the assault . . . and backing up more . . . until *Aramis made a mistake.* Joey saw a gap in the older rat's defenses—he was leaving the left side of his stomach unguarded. Like a flash, Joey jabbed Ratscalibur at the gap. . . .

. . . and Aramis calmly flicked the sword out of Joey's hand. Ratscalibur clattered away, landing by the fallen body of poor Parsifur.

Joey stood there, empty-handed, looking at Sir Aramis, who was regarding him coolly. "Remarkable," said Sir Aramis. "You execute a perfect Moustoffsky Cross, yet you fall for a simple Rat-bane Gambit."

"I guess I still have a lot to learn," said Joey.

"Yes," said Sir Aramis. "It's a pity you'll never have a chance to learn it." He raised up his sword to strike the killing blow, but Joey dropped to the ground and scrambled on all fours over to Ratscalibur. If he was going to die, he was going to die with his sword in his hand.

As he reached for his blade, he came face-to-face with Sir Parsifur, whose little eyes were shiny and open and unblinking.

Joey heard Sir Aramis's footsteps bearing down on him, knew the villainous knight was standing over him, about to stab him in the back. And at that moment he decided he would not die now. Not on his knees. With his eyes locked on Parsifur's, he reached out, felt Ratscalibur in his grasp, then turned and leaped up into the jaws of death.

SIR ARAMIS was knocked on his back by Joey's flying leap. He jumped back to his feet, but he seemed surprised by Joey's new ferocity.

"Well, well," he said, "there's some fight in y—" But Joey didn't let him finish. He jabbed furiously at the traitorous vizier, pushing forward relentlessly. Ratscalibur moved ten times faster than before. It felt lighter, swifter in his grasp. It danced around Sir Aramis's body like a swarm of bees.

It was Aramis's turn to back up and back up. He was under too much stress to say anything now. His brow was wrinkled with concentration. And something else.

Fear.

That only made Joey bolder. He pressed forward, ever forward.

Sir Aramis kept blocking his blows—*click clack click*—but he was clearly getting tired. His sword was moving slower, and slower. . . .

And then Aramis couldn't back up any farther. His back was pressed to the garbage can outside the apartment window. Joey made a powerful lunge . . . and the sword flew from Aramis's hand. Joey lunged once more, and Aramis ducked beneath the blow. He dropped to the ground at Joey's feet, as Joey's sword banged into the garbage can with *claaaaang.*

Joey looked down at the helpless warrior. There was not a trace of pride on Sir Aramis's face anymore. Now all that Joey could see was terror. The sewer rats, who had been cheering Aramis on, fell suddenly silent, as they realized that their leader was beaten. "Do you give up?" asked Joey.

"What?" said Aramis. "What? No, no . . . it can't be. This isn't supposed to happen. . . ."

"But it's happening," said Joey. "Do you give up?"

Sir Aramis opened his mouth to say something, but nothing came out. His jaw worked up and down, uselessly.

"Do you give up?"

Again, Aramis opened his mouth uselessly, without making a sound. But then a sly look came into his eye. He turned his face to the crowd of water rats watching them and yelled, "Kill him!"

"What?" said Joey.

"Kill him, my Under-Realmers! Destroy the High-Realmer! Tear him limb from limb!"

The Under-Realmers hesitated. This seemed a little low, even for them.

"Victory is still in our grasp!" Aramis screamed in a piercing, panicked high wail, *"Kill him!"*

That was all the encouragement they needed. The wild rats

and the crows that had remained now swooped in for the kill. Joey turned to face his assassins and put his back to the garbage can.

"You're not a knight," he said to Aramis. "You don't have any honor."

"I don't want *honor*," laughed Aramis, with a sick snicker. "I want a crown."

The sewer rats, with the Berzerkers in the lead, were in Joey's face now. Taunting, feinting, grabbing.

Joey kept swinging his sword, desperately, trying to keep them away for just a few more seconds . . . just a few more seconds . . . he couldn't let them win *yet*.

And that's when everything started *shaking*.

Wait—not everything. Just the garbage can at Joey's back. Shaking and rattling and bouncing like it was alive, leaning and teetering till it seemed like it would fall over any second. *Was it haunted?* The rats backed off a little, alarmed. The crows flapped away.

"Don't stop now!" yelled Aramis, still crouched on the ground. "Kill him!"

The garbage can came to a sudden stop. It was completely quiet again, like a garbage can should be.

"See?" yelled Aramis. "See? It stopped. It was nothing. It was—"

Clangggggg! The lid shot off the garbage can like a cannon going off. A loud voice boomed out from inside the can. "Under-Realmers. Go back. Go back to your sewers and sludge."

The voice sounded a little familiar to Joey. It must have sounded familiar to Aramis, too, because he cringed and said, "No. No, it can't be. . . ."

"Crows," said the stern voice, "go back to your trees and your garbage dumps. Go. Go now!"

Aramis looked at Joey accusingly, "But you said . . . *you said*—"

"This is your final warning," boomed the voice.

"Who is it?"

"You really don't know?" said Aramis pathetically. He whispered, "It's . . . it's *Gondorff*. Gondorff the Gray."

"No," said the voice, in its loudest tone yet, as a medium-sized rat covered in curly, wild red fur climbed out of the garbage can and perched on the rim. "No. It's now *Gondorff the Red*."

MOST OF THE wild rats ran screaming for the nearest sewer opening.

A few of the crazier ones, mostly Berzerkers, tried to rush Gondorff, throwing spears as they ran, while some crows dived down at him.

Gondorff made a calm gesture with one of his paws. The marauding rats and crows fell straight down, like sand bags. *Thump. Thump. Thump thump thump.*

Gondorff hopped down off the garbage can and walked over to Joey. Joey looked at the sidewalk, littered with fallen crows and wild rats. "Are they dead?"

The red Ragician chuckled. "They'll wish they were when they wake up."

Joey looked Gondorff in the face. Yes, despite the red curls, and the evident strength in this rat, the eyes were the same. This was the same rat Uncle Patrick had given him. "But how are you . . . ?"

"*Magic*," said Gondorff.

"You mean *Ragic*?"

"No, I mean *Magic*. It's immensely powerful. But terribly sad." He gazed up at the apartment window. "They never know when they're using it."

Joey looked at the window where Mom was, then back down at Gondorff. For the first time, he realized that Gondorff's fur was now the exact same shade as Mom's hair. . . .

Joey realized that all of these questions could wait. "Aramis!" said Joey. "He—" Joey looked down and saw that the vizier had made his escape. "He's gone."

"He won't get far."

"And my friends! The princess! They're all—"

Gondorff laid a comforting arm on Joey's shoulder. "They're all still alive. And now . . ." Gondorff closed his eyes, made a gesture with his hand, and grunted. "Now they're all healed, as well."

Behind them there was a clatter as the fallen garbage-can lids of the fort were knocked aside. Brutilda and Uncle Patrick sprang up, looking like they'd just come back from vacation. And leaping onto Brutilda's back was a spritely, wide-awake—

"Yislene!" cried Joey.

"Can someone please bring me a chicken bone?" she yelled. "A ladybug lung? Anything? I'm *starving*."

Brutilda scrounged in the garbage to get something tasty for her mistress. Uncle Patrick hugged Joey. "We made it, honcho."

"Yes, we . . ." he said, then stopped. "But Parsifur."

He looked. The little white rat lay motionless in an enormous puddle of blood. Completely still. Like a broken toy.

And then he sighed.

And then he wriggled a little, this way, then that. And he slowly got to his feet, like a zombie coming to life. He stretched his arms. . . . He stretched his legs. . . . He opened his mouth, and he giggled, "*Hee-hee-hee*." He grabbed the sword that was by his feet and walked over to his friends.

"It's been a while, Gondorff," he said, seemingly unsurprised. "I see you've been going to the beauty parlor."

Gondorff growled.

"What took you so long?" asked Joey.

Parsifur smiled. "I had a longer way to come back, I imagine." Joey hugged the giggling knight. "Now, Sir Joey," said Parsifur, "I need you to do something for me."

"What's that?"

"Give me back my sword."

"Your . . ." Joey looked down at the sword in his hand. It wasn't Ratscalibur. It was Parsifur's straightened paper clip. He must have grabbed it when Aramis knocked Ratscalibur out of his hand. No wonder it had felt so light when he was fighting. . . .

"A spork's a marvelous weapon," said Parsifur. "But a bit heavy for warriors our size, I tend to think."

Joey didn't understand. "If I wasn't fighting with Ratscalibur, how did I . . . ?"

"I guess the blade's not the only one with power, is it?" said Parsifur. "Now kindly return my sword. *Hee-hee-hee*."

39

THE SUN SEEMED to shine brighter in Ravalon than it had before. It wasn't just because there weren't any crows overhead. *It's because there isn't the threat of crows either,* thought Joey.

As the heroes walked back into the town square, a simultaneous whoop and laugh and *cheer* erupted from the gathered crowd. Joey was hugged and kissed and squeezed till he felt like he was fighting the Under-Realmers all over again.

"That's my lad!" said the rat mother who'd saved him—could it have been only two days ago? "That's my lad! He's eaten acorns from my own larder!" She pinched his cheeks till he thought they'd fall off. Her pink babies swarmed over Joey like happy puppies. . . .

"The look on your face," laughed Parsifur, just before he was knocked to the ground by a black hurricane. When Joey glanced down, he saw Parsifur lying on his back—and Drattleby kissing him on the cheeks!

"Well done, old man! Well done!" said the black knight. "All is forgiven!"

Parsifur suffered in silence for a moment before grunting, "I think I liked it better when we were enemies."

But this time it was Drattleby who giggled. *Haw-haw-haw.*

An iron grip went around Joey's arm. He recognized it immediately: Brutilda. "Come," she said. "The king is waiting." The crowd—and guards—parted as the little procession of heroes made its way into the palace.

Everything was different in the throne room now. Everything felt brighter, cleaner. But it might have just felt brighter and cleaner because King Uther was so different. He still sat in the same throne, but now he glowed with strength and health and wisdom. His leg was still injured, but it didn't look like that bothered him anymore. He chuckled as Yislene ran into the room and threw herself around his neck. "Daddy!" Then he turned to Joey and Patrick.

"My kingdom owes you its eternal gratitude."

Joey didn't know what to say. Luckily, Uncle Patrick did. "Our pleasure, Your Majesty."

"Please kneel, so that I can bestow upon you this small token of my thanks."

Joey and Patrick got to their knees. King Uther tapped them on the shoulders with his sword and said, "For service to this kingdom, and the entire Low Realm in general, I dub thee Sir Joey Stump-Tail and Sir Patrick Tiger-Tusk."

Parsifur had been calling Joey Sir Joey for a while now, but it was nice to make it official.

When Joey and Patrick stood up, their friends were all around

them to slap their backs and hug them. Then King Uther did something unprecedented. He stood up, teetering on his lame leg, and shook Joey's hand. "This is for giving me my mind back."

Gondorff grimaced. "I'll never forgive myself for not seeing the signs of Squirrelin's cursed *Squagic* on you."

"Don't blame yourself, Red," said Parsifur. "He fooled us all."

They'd already sent a scouting party to Squirrelin's lair and found the old oak deserted. Nutkin and Squirrelin were gone. And they'd had to leave behind Squirrelin's acorns and his warehouse full of food. Joey could only imagine how much that must have pained the old Squagician. Probably more than losing his powers.

"And . . . the other one?" Uther asked. He couldn't bring himself to say his former vizier's name.

Gondorff grimaced again. "There's still no trace, Your Majesty." The trail of Aramis's smell had reached a little ways away from the final battle and then suddenly disappeared. Now no one could pick it up again. When Joey asked his nose, *Where's Aramis?* and sniffed, all he got was burning spice. Yislene said it was possible to make your smell vanish if you submerged it within a stronger smell. But no one could disappear forever.

Actually, Joey hoped Aramis *would* disappear forever. Squirrelin too, while he was at it. No good could ever come from seeing those two again.

"Now," said King Uther, "must you really leave so soon? I would be delighted to show you a proper feast."

"And we'd be delighted to eat it, Your Majesty," said Uncle Patrick. "But we need to get home as fast as possible."

"Definitely," said Joey. He turned and handed Ratscalibur to Brutilda. "Here, brave Brutilda, is a gift for you. It's better for someone your size, anyway."

Brutilda took the blade and said, "I'm not worthy to carry it. But I'll care for it until you return."

"But I'm not coming back," said Joey.

"*Hee-hee-hee*, that's what you think," said Parsifur, as he squeezed Joey from behind. Something hot and wet tickled Joey's ankles, and without even looking down, Joey said, "Get out of the throne room, Chequers." The cat yowled with displeasure, but Joey laughed and patted her nose. "I'm just kidding, Checky."

"Jffy, Mgggblllb." That was Yislene trying to talk with a mouth full of Cheetos. She'd been eating nonstop since they'd returned. She swallowed, hard, and said, "Sir Joey, I . . ." Then she stopped. She tried to start again, "I just, I want . . . I just—"

Whatever she wanted to say, it wouldn't come out. She started to breathe more heavily, like she was having a panic attack. "Princess," said Joey, "are you okay? What's—"

Without warning, Yislene leaned in, kissed Joey on the mouth, and ran out of the room. Joey stood there, dazed.

"Well," said Uncle Patrick, "I guess she—"

At that moment Brutilda leaned in, kissed Patrick on the mouth, and ran out the same door as Yislene.

Joey and Uncle Patrick just stood there, looking at each other, as everyone else in the room laughed. "I think," said Joey, "I think

I have a crush on a rat."

Uncle Patrick sighed and muttered under his breath, "Better that than a guinea pig."

From out in the hallway, a deep voice boomed, "I have ears."

Gondorff cleared his throat. "Are you ready?"

Joey and Patrick shared a look. They were.

"Hold out your right paws."

They did so.

"Now. Do you give me these paws willingly?"

THEY HAD TO KNOCK on the door because neither of them had a key. Mom had a dead look on her face when she opened the door, until she saw Uncle Patrick. She saw him first, because he was so big. Her face filled with amazement, "Patrick!" she said.

Then she looked down and saw Joey. Then it was, "Joey!" and "*Joey Joey Joey!*" as she knelt on the floor and cried and hugged and kissed him. "Are you okay?"

"I'm fine, Mom, I'm fine," said Joey, who hugged and kissed her back.

Mom stood up and hugged Uncle Patrick. Then she slapped him across the face, hard. "Where *were* you?" she said.

Uncle Patrick and Joey shared a look. "It's . . . kind of hard to explain, Sis."

Mom looked at them. And then she smiled and said, "Then don't. Not yet." And she bent down to hug Joey some more. She was happy, but she almost seemed kind of lost, like she couldn't quite believe this was really happening.

Uncle Patrick ran inside to get the coffee maker started. Joey put his arm around Mom's waist and walked her to the couch. They sat down with their arms around each other, and Joey was pretty sure at that moment that they would never, ever let each other go again. "I can't believe it. . . ." Mom said, over and over again. But it was like her voice still wasn't quite her own.

Patrick came in from the kitchen, with a cup of coffee for Mom (and a can of beer for himself). He pushed the mug into her hands, but it was like she didn't know what to do with it. So Joey helped her put it to her lips, and that act of normalcy—just sitting on the couch, drinking coffee like always—somehow broke the spell that had come over her. Her complexion brightened. Her hair regained its bounce. She stared deep into Joey's eyes and said, "You're grounded."

Joey stared right back and said, "That sounds great."

Uncle Patrick sat down next to them. "This is a nice couch," he said.

Joey hadn't wanted to move to the city. He had been comfortable back in his old town. He knew who everybody was, and he spoke the same language as everyone there. It wasn't as loud there. It wasn't as crowded. It wasn't as smelly.

But his mom had gotten a job here, in the city. It was a better job, and she'd taken it because it was better for Joey. For the first time Joey realized that moving to the city was probably pretty scary for *Mom*, too. . . .

Maybe he did have heroes in his family.

"What are you thinking about, kiddo?" asked Mom, as she brushed Joey's bangs out of his eyes.

Joey looked around. He looked at the iron bars on the window. He could almost see the waves of late-summer heat bouncing off the sidewalk. It was all out there. The traffic, and the cockroaches, and the dust, and the rats . . .

"I'm thinking that there's a lot of scary things here." Mom nodded. Then Joey said, "But I'm not going to be scared of them."

Mom smiled. "Me neither," she said.

Joey decided that if the boy across the street waved again, he would wave back.

a few
bLocks away

WRUNDEL TURNED *in her bed of garbage. She licked her paw where Parsifur had stabbed her, and yowled. It still hurt.*

A brown- and gray-flecked paw reached up and scratched her ear, to comfort her. It was dark here, and oily . . . but he knew his special pet's smell would hide him from his enemies.

His enemies, *he thought.* They should be his subjects. At this moment, he should be their king.

Ah, well. He would wait. And he would plot. He had done it before.

"Soon, my sweet, soon," *said the rat.* "Soon, we will have our revenge."

Wrundel purred.

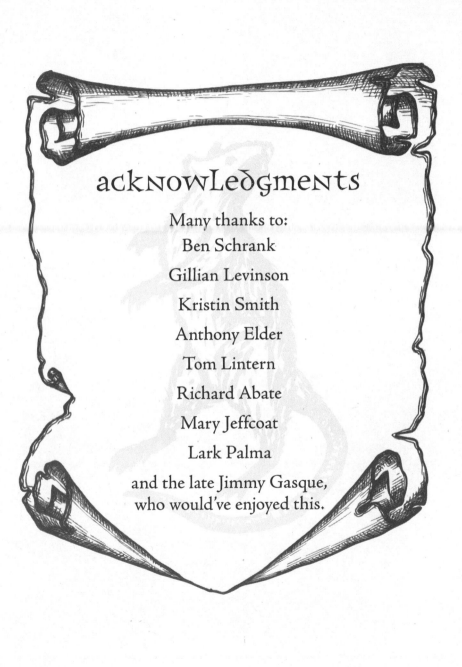

acknowledgments

Many thanks to:

Ben Schrank

Gillian Levinson

Kristin Smith

Anthony Elder

Tom Lintern

Richard Abate

Mary Jeffcoat

Lark Palma

and the late Jimmy Gasque, who would've enjoyed this.

LIKED JOEY?

Meet Oliver Watson.
He doesn't turn into a rat, but he
does run for class president.

And yeah, he's also an evil genius.

Turn the page for a peek at his story . . .

CHAPTER 1.
FEAR ME

Someday you will beg for the honor of licking my feet. You will get down on your stupid, worthless knees and beg, "Please, sir! Please! Let me lick the diseased dog dung from between your toes." (I will be standing barefoot in the dung of diseased dogs—just to make it grosser for you.) And if I am in a good mood and am not too disgusted by your stupid, wormy tears or your stupid, scrunched-up face, I will allow you the signal honor of licking my feet clean. Even though you don't deserve it.

But that's all in the future. At the moment, I'm in the seventh grade.

In fact, at this *precise* moment, I am in Mr. Moorhead's English class as he prattles on about *Fahrenheit 451*. Moorhead considers himself a "cool" teacher (*see plate 1*). That means he still wears the clothes he wore in college. Unfortunately for Moorhead, college was ten years and twenty pounds ago. His legs look like a pair of light-blue water balloons, stuffed as they are into too-tight jeans. He can't get all the buttons on his crotch to

PLATE 1: Moorhead considers himself a "cool" teacher.

stay fastened anymore (*Way cool, Mr. M!*), and he wears plaid flannel shirts that gape open over his salmon-pink belly. He's balding, but he thinks if he leaves his hair messy enough, we won't notice. He also keeps a pack of cigarettes in the pocket over his heart. This is supposed to say, "I am a teacher, but I'm not a saint." In reality, it just makes his saggy man-breasts look bigger. It also says, "I smell bad."[1]

Moorhead is one of those sad people who go into teaching so they can be worshipped by the only people sadder than they are—students. Prime example: Pammy Quattlebaum, so-called smart girl and insufferable butt-lick, who sits in the front row, nodding her massive head frequently to show Moorhead that not only has she done the reading, she understands *exactly* what he's saying.

Meanwhile, I am in the back of the room, drawing pictures of bunny rabbits on my binder.

Moorhead is way too cool to lecture standing up or sitting down. Instead, he lounges sexily against his desk, elbow propped on the dictionary, as he lays his knowledge on us. "The book depicts a world turned upside down." (Pammy nods.) "A world where firemen don't put out fires—they set them." (Pammy nods again, more emphatically.) "A world where the most dangerous weapon you can own"—here he holds up his copy of

---

1. Which he does.

Fahrenheit 451—"is a book." (Pammy nods so hard I can hear her tiny brain rattle, like a popcorn kernel in a jelly jar.)

Moorhead, simulating deep thought, runs his fingers through the pubic growth that decorates his scalp. "What do you think? Are books dangerous? Are they... *powerful*?"

Pammy surges out of her seat, arm straining for the sky. She will apparently pee herself if she's not allowed to answer this question.

But Moorhead's eyes slide over to me. "What do you think, Oliver?"

Pammy shoots me a dirty look. Some of my other class-mates giggle and don't bother trying to hide it. Randy Sparks, the Most Pathetic Boy in School, stops licking dried peanut butter off his glasses long enough to give me a sympathetic smile.

Moorhead grins like he's made a great joke. I am fairly certain I was only assigned to this class—which is far beyond my tested reading level—so he'd have someone to make fun of (besides Randy, of course).

I make him say my name again before I answer, "I don't know."

Moorhead's face crumples with disappointment, but his eyes shine with satisfaction. "Oliver. Didn't you do the reading?"

I shake my head sadly. Moorhead sighs. He looks like he wants to cry for me. Or burst out laughing. It's like his brain can't decide.

Actually, I read the book when I was two. And even *then* I knew it was regurgitated bird pap, fit only for morons and seventh graders. In case you're lucky enough to have escaped it, *Fahrenheit 451* is one of those books that is about how *amazing* books are and how *wonderful* the people who *write* books are. Writers love writing books like this, and for some reason, we let them get away with it. It's like someone producing a TV show called *TV Shows Are the Best and the People Who Make Them Are Geniuses.*[2]

In *Fahrenheit 451*, books are illegal (because they're so powerful) and a fireman's job is to burn all the books he can find in big bonfires. This is supposed to blow your freaking mind.[3]

Moorhead walks back to my lonely little desk and puts a comforting hand on my shoulder. "It's too bad you skipped

---

2. Probably the name of Aaron Sorkin's next project. Ha.

3. I plan on having a *Fahrenheit 451* party one day. To get in, you have to bring a copy of *Fahrenheit 451*. Then we build a big fire and . . . well, you do the math.

it, big guy. Because it happens to be one of the best books written in the past century."

His furry fingers rest on my shoulder like caterpillars. I decide not to bite them. One of the best books of the century? *Fahrenheit 451* doesn't rank as one of the best birdcage liners of the century.

And besides—even if it were "*one* of the best books"... is that anything to brag about? Wouldn't it look kind of drab and shabby when compared to the book that's the actual best?

It doesn't pay to be good at something unless you are the absolute best at it. Otherwise, you'll eventually go up against someone who can beat you. That is why I do not try to play soccer, sing in the school chorus, or dance, even though I am moderately talented at all of these things. I concentrate on what I am good at: being a genius.

I am the greatest genius in the universe. I am the greatest genius in the history of the universe. Plus, I am unceasingly, unreservedly, unspeakably evil. Making me *the most powerful force for evil ever created.*

And poor Mr. Moorhead thinks I'm the dumbest boy in his English class.

The bell rings. Moorhead gives me one last pitying glance, then strolls back to the board. "Read the next chapter for tomorrow, people. And remember—nominations for student council have to be submitted at your next homeroom." He smiles at Jack Chapman, who lowers his handsome head modestly and runs a bashful hand through his soft and kinky hair. Jack exits with the throng, enduring much backslapping and people yelling, "You got my vote, Jack." I pretend to fumble with my books so I can see what happens next.

It's lunchtime. As always, Moorhead reaches into his shirt pocket for his pack of cigarettes and shakes one out. He does this right after class, even though he can't smoke in the classroom, even though he can't smoke in the school. He must walk a legally mandated ten yards off school property before he can smoke his death stick. But he always pulls it out right after class.

He looks at the cigarette with longing . . . then with surprise. He holds it close to his weak, middle-aged eyes. There's a message typed neatly on the little tube:

.

Moorhead stares at the cigarette a moment, then looks up with suspicion and fury. But the only people he sees are me and Pammy, who is also dawdling, but for very different reasons.[4]

---

4. She wants him to read a poem she wrote about lowering carbon emissions. Absolute garbage. Sample verse: *Carbon credits are the answer/ To our planet's dreaded cancer.*

Pammy gives him a simpering smile, which he ignores. I, halfwit that I am, am singing a song to myself as I look for my pencil under the desk. The only words to the song are *"Three, please. Can I see threeeee pretty pictures. ...."* Moorhead gives me a scornful glance before hurrying out of the room.

But the look of terror on his face in that single, unguarded moment of surprise is truly a beautiful, beautiful thing.

There will be three full-color photographs of that moment waiting for me by the time I get to my locker.